Battle of
Dreamcast Mountain

Diane Banham

Book Two

The Dream Drifters Series

Battle of
Dreamcast Mountain

Imagination can take you anywhere

Cover design by Leanne Brown at Sirenic Creations

To all of life's dreamers.

Dream, imagine & believe

CHAPTER 1

Maisie

Maisie woke with a jolt as the car stopped and her head bumped against the window. Rubbing her sleepy eyes, she looked around confused, where was she? The last thing she remembered was mum saying good night and turning out the light. How had she got into the car?

"Here we are Maisie, how exciting," said mum as a hand reached in the open door and helped her from her seat.

Her mind in a jumble Maisie climbed out of the car. She did not recognize this place or any of the children running around but strangely she knew exactly where it was, SCHOOL.

Nervously twiddling one brown plait whilst fidgeting with her pink unicorn rucksack Maisie walked into the playground. Deep down inside her tummy she had an awful sinking feeling so fixing her eyes firmly on her feet she grasped mum's hand tightly.

Through her downturned eyes, she saw pair after pair of shiny new shoes run by when suddenly she spotted something strange. A pair of shoeless feet ran past that were brown and hairy with long toes and had the grubbiest toenails she had ever seen. Another and another until all the shoes were gone and instead, she stood surrounded by brown hairy feet.

"Look at all the wonderful children, you can make so many new friends," said Mum reassuringly.

Slowly a confused Maisie lifted her head when suddenly someone bumped into her.

"Oh, I'm so sorry" she apologised, even though it was not her fault she thought it good manners. Looking up she expected to see the glowing face of an excited child but to her horror, she stood face to face with a large monkey. It had brown fur, big ears, and a long tail that wiggled as it blew a loud wet raspberry in her face and ran away.

Gasping in shock Maisie turned to Mum, but where was she? Mum had vanished and the entire playground was now bursting with monkeys making the loudest commotion she had ever heard.

Maisie clasped her hands over her ringing ears as she desperately searched for Mum when looking down, she realised she was not wearing her school uniform. Under the unicorn rucksack, she was dressed in her favourite pyjamas, dressing gown, and slippers. Her heart began to thump louder and louder as she felt the butterflies in her stomach rising. What was happening?

DING A LING A LING A LING!!!

A loud bell rang out across the playground instantly stopping the monkey's games. In complete chaos, they raced across the playground towards the large school doors that were opening.

Before Maisie knew what was happening two monkeys appeared and excitedly grabbed her hands, dragging her with them.

"NO STOP IT LET ME GO" she cried in terror.

Maisie pulled back, but they were so strong, and as they pulled her inside the doors slammed shut with a loud *BANG!*

Frantically she grabbed the door handle and tried with all her might to open them, but they would not budge. Then from somewhere behind, there came a low growl making the hairs on her neck stand on end as a chill of fear trickled down her back. Gradually Maisie turned around, what was making that noise?

Through her tear filled eyes, she could just make out a long corridor smothered in vines that moved as if they were alive. It was so quiet Maisie's heartbeat pounded in her ears as the noisy monkeys seemed to have vanished into thin air.

Black and white tiles lined the floor and along either side stood rows of closed doors with frosted glass in the top. Behind four of the doors, the lights were on and a long light above flickered with a *plink, plink, plink*.

THUMP, something hit Maisie's sleeve and as she looked down a shiny black beetle scuttled into view looking at her curiously.

"GET OFF, GET OFF" Maisie squealed shaking her arm when suddenly, the beetle curled up into a black ball and bounced away. "What's happening I don't understand," she sobbed as the fear inside her began to grow.

A rustling sound behind startled her and turning back towards the doors she was faced with a wall of vines. The doors to the outside world had gone.

****

Deep at the bottom of Maisie's rucksack, squashed in tightly by her new glittery pencil case, the three tiny Dream Drifters and their faithful red Dream Dragon Ember hid.

"All I'm saying is why couldn't we have hidden in the fluffy dressing gown pocket or hood, that's what I want to know?" complained Snitch. "It's a bit of a squeeze in here and not very comfortable" he mumbled as Maisie's pencil case nudged towards him.

"Oh, Snitch *please* be quiet" sighed Noggin "you know Maisie doesn't know we're here, and this is the safest place to hide."

Fitz, the team leader, was balancing carefully at the top peeping out to see the jungle corridor beyond.

"Anything yet?" asked Noggin pushing the pencil case away with her foot and covering her boot with glitter.

"Not yet, well not really" Fitz whispered down. "Just a lot of screaming monkeys, bouncing beetles, and a jungle in the school" he replied calmly.

"A *what* and a *what*?" squeaked Snitch in horror his white spiky hair standing even more on end than usual. "Can't we just capture it now and go home?"

13

"Snitch you know as well as we do that we have to wait until we get to the centre of the nightmare, the thing that's the most terrifying to Maisie before we can catch it" replied Noggin.

"If we are too early, we risk not trapping it at all and the nightmare will continue for Maisie until she wakes," continued Fitz. "Then we will have to come back and do it all again when she is next asleep, and I'm guessing you won't want to do that?"

"No, I sure don't" grumbled Snitch crossly shoving Embers warm scaly foot out of his face.

****

Since the door to the outside world was now a mass of creeping vines Maisie had no choice but to move along the corridor.

"There must be way out down here" she whispered to herself wiping her eyes on her dressing gown sleeve. Placing her feet carefully in the gaps between vines, Maisie began to cautiously walk forward when *squelch* she felt something soft under her slipper.

"Oh no, not monkey poo please" she whispered to herself as she lifted her foot. Laying on the jungle floor was a large rainbow coloured slug, squashed flat in the shape of Maisie's slipper print.

"Oh no, I've killed it" she wailed bending down in alarm, but to her utter surprise, the footprint shaped slug turned its eyes to look at her and carried on its merry way.

Maisie watched in fascination as it reached a small hollow vine on the floor and squeezed inside. When it eventually appeared out the other end (which took a while as slugs are slow, even magical rainbow coloured ones) it was long and thin identical to the hole in the vine it had crawled through.

"Now that's a good trick, Squidgeable Slugs," she said smiling as it slipped away leaving a trail of purple glittery slime.

Carefully Maisie continued along the corridor, stepping over slugs and dodging bouncing beetles until she stopped level with the first lit door. Behind the frosted glass, Maisie saw movement.

"There's someone in there, maybe they could help me?" Running for the door she grabbed the handle and without thinking threw it wide open.

"Oh no, hold on tight" called Fitz to the others, "this could get a bit choppy."

At first, the classroom looked empty with row upon row of desks and chairs all facing a blackboard. Then in the quiet, came a low growl like the one she had heard in the corridor outside.

16

Across the room, an enormous wolf appeared. With fur as white as snow and flickering orange eyes, it leapt onto a desktop. Sharp claws click-clacked and a strong tail swished as it prowled around the desks hunting its prey. Maisie froze in fear.

"What was that?" called Snitch.

"Oh, err nothing" fibbed Fitz as he watched the creature stop and turn to face them licking its lips with a huge pink tongue.

"He's fibbing" whispered Snitch to Noggin, "I know it I can feel Maisie shaking."

"Of course, he is silly, he always fibs to you in case you *freak out*" she replied looking at Ember squashed in with a Pug keyring dangling on her head.

The wolf looked at Maisie for a moment tipping its head to one side as if thinking, then it began to snarl scrunching up its nose and curling its lips to

17

reveal its dagger like teeth. With a piercing howl, it sprang from the desk, lunging directly at the frightened girl stood outside.

"MAISIE THE DOOR, THE DOOR, CLOSE THE DOOR" screamed Fitz in the terrified girl's ear.

Obeying the voice in her head Maisie reached in and grabbed the door handle, slamming it shut just as the wolf reached them. The mighty beast hit the closed door with a *THUD* making it shudder. The room beyond fell silent and the light went out.

Maisie stumbled back in shock and panic. She turned to run but her foot caught in a vine and as she dropped to her knees the unicorn rucksack plunged forward.

"WHOOOAAA" wailed Fitz as without warning he lost his grip and shot out of the rucksack. Flying over Maisie's shoulder he just managed to grab the ribbon on one of her plaits to stop himself hitting the floor. Maisie looked down at the tiny person swinging from her hair as she puffed in fright.

"Hi Maisie," said Fitz a little embarrassed.

"Hi" replied Maisie staring at him her eyes wide with fear.

"Any chance you could help me down?" he asked looking towards the floor.

Maisie lifted her hand and lowered Fitz to the floor where he jumped off and stood on the nearest vine.

"Thanks," he said adjusting his backpack and looking up at her.

"Who are you and where did you come from?" asked Maisie studying the tiny person with his black mop of hair, rosy cheeks, and kind face before placing her rucksack on the floor beside them.

"I'm Fitz and I know you don't remember me, but trust me we have met many times before."

CHAPTER 2

Slishy Sloshy

The pink unicorn rucksack started to squirm with grunts and groans followed by muffled voices coming from inside.

"Don't rush me I'm going as fast as I can, I have a pencil case on my head."

"Well, get a move on it's not nice being trapped under your smelly bottom you know."

Maisie stared at it, a little afraid of what might pop out when there appeared a small red dragons face. The tiny dragon wriggled and crawled until she was out of the bag, and with a shake to stretch her crumpled wings flew down to join Fitz.

"This is Ember our Dream Dragon," he said with a pat to her neck as she gave a puff of smoke.

"Hey, what about us?" as Noggin with her red stuck up hair, and Snitch with his glasses on wonky clambered ungracefully from the bag and climbed down to join them.

Fitz made the introductions as Maisie gazed at the three tiny people and the dragon before her and wondered if she was dreaming or in fact, they were real.

Snitch was a little smaller than the others with a mass of white stuck up hair like he had a fright. He was wearing a pair of black gloves and thick black rimmed glasses that magnified his eyes, so they looked enormous compared to his head.

Noggin had the most incredible red wild hair that almost matched Ember's scales and green eyes with freckles sprinkled across her nose. Around her waist hung a large brown belt that had masses of pockets and items hanging from it. Maisie did not know what they were all for, but they looked fascinating.

"Boy am I glad to be out of there" moaned Snitch straightening his glasses and ruffling his squashed hair.

"So, fibber Fitz what was that noise?" asked Noggin her eyebrows raised and hands on hips.

"It didn't sound like nothing to me that's for sure," said Snitch.

"A wolf, a huge mean wolf that tried to eat me in that classroom there," said Maisie pointing at the door.

"A wolf, that tried to eat you. Well that's ok I thought it might be something *really scary*" said Snitch punching Fitz in the arm. "It can't get out can it?" he whispered.

"No, I shut it in tight," said Maisie proudly.

23

From further along the corridor there was a loud *slosh.* Through the glass on the next lit door ripples and shimmers appeared in the classroom light.

Maisie's heart started to thump and the whirly panic of butterflies in her stomach came back again.

"Please tell me we don't have to open that door?" she asked Fitz as tears began to fill her eyes.

"Maisie you're dreaming," said Noggin grasping her little finger in both her tiny hands. "It's okay, none of this is real and we are here to help you, but you have to trust us. Can you do that for me?"

Maisie nodded, at least it made sense now, she was dreaming and not going crazy, phew!

"Maisie what exactly are you scared of?" asked Fitz.

"Oh well, lots of things, wolves eating me being one of them," she said turning and looking back at the door behind her.

"Okay, anything else? Is there something that scares you more than all the others put together?"

"Well, my brother says I'm afraid of everything" she huffed. "There is one thing though" shuddered Maisie. "They scare me so much I-I-I can't even say the word."

"By chance do they maybe involve water?" asked Snitch looking in the direction of the slishy sloshy door as the sound got louder and louder.

SLISH-SLOSH-SLISH-SLOSH-SLISH!!

Maisie shook her head.

"Well, that door certainly wants us to open it," said Fitz "and at least whatever's back there can't be the thing you're most scared off." Maisie stood up and took a deep breath trying to calm her panic.

With Snitch and Ember safely in her pocket and Fitz and Noggin sitting on her shoulders, Maisie walked down the corridor towards the door.

"We will be right here with you and remember just shut the door and whatever is in there can't get you," said Noggin. "Remember, it's just a dream and you're in control."

As Maisie stood looking at the door, she noticed water seeping from its edges and gathering on the floor. Playing in it were tiny frogs but they were no ordinary frogs, they were completely clear as if made from glass. As they glinted in the reflecting watery light Maisie bent down to touch one. *PLINK*... it shattered into pieces making her gasp in shock.

"Oh no I've broken it," she cried in horror her hand to her mouth. As they watched in amazement the four pieces started to wriggle as slowly each one grew legs and transformed into a new frog.

"Now that's clever, aww look how cute they are" gushed Noggin as the tiny new frogs hopped around.

SLISH-SLOSH-SLISH-SLOSH the room was calling.

Maisie grasped the cold door handle in her trembling hand. She opened it a little, then gave it a small push to reveal a classroom much like the wolf's, only this one was completely underwater. Oddly, the water did not rush out of the open door but remained in the room from ceiling to floor.

"Maisie w-w-what are you s-s-scared of that l-l-lives underwater?" stammered Snitch dropping a little further down into her pocket to hide.

"Oh no," gasped Maisie under her breath suddenly remembering.

"Oh no, what?" asked Fitz and Noggin together.

"SHARKS" cried Maisie as the biggest, two headed shark they had ever seen swam straight towards her, both mouths wide open with rows of razor teeth and four black beady eyes shining.

"*DOOR*" screamed Fitz as Noggin grabbed her grappling hook from her belt and shot it through the water to the handle. With an almighty yank, it slammed shut *SPLASH*, soaking them all in cold salty seawater. A menacing dark finned shadow drifted across the glass for a moment then swam out of sight.

The light inside went off as they stood dripping wet with glass frogs dangling from Maisie's dressing gown belt.

"*TWO HEADS!!!*" cried Snitch in shock his head in his hands. "*WHY TWO HEADS MAISIE????*" as he slid down deep in her pocket and out of sight.

28

"I don't know, maybe one head wasn't scary enough" she replied.

Noggin started to chuckle softly at first then louder and louder followed by Fitz, then Maisie joined in until all three were laughing so hard it hurt.

"Ember is he all right in there?" asked Maisie looking down at the dragon in her pocket.

Ember looked down at the wet and cross Snitch sulking at the bottom and nodded.

"Two lights left," said Noggin looking along the corridor, "one there and that one right at the very end."

Maisie walked along the corridor and stopped before the next lit door. She put her ear to it and listened, nothing, but as she reached for the handle there came a cry from Fitz.

"Wait, Maisie, wait a second. Snitch get your grumpy bottom up here this instant" he called down to the pocket, but Snitch didn't move as he was still moping.

"I think a little encouragement is needed," said Noggin winking at Ember as the dragon grinned and disappeared. Gradually puffs of smoke started to drift from the pocket, then Maisie started to get a slight tingly warm feeling on her leg.

"Wait for it, any second now" smirked Noggin.

"*OOOOOWWWWW* all right, all right keep your hot smelly breath to yourself" coughed Snitch as he popped out the top with smoke swirling around his head and fogged up glasses.

"Nice of you to decide to join us," said Fitz. "Now can you see what's inside before we open the door?"

"I can try but everything's wet" huffed Snitch clapping his sopping gloves together with a wet *slap*. There was a crackle of light from his gloves and glasses and to Maisie's amazement there appeared a keyboard made from light. Unfortunately, it only lasted for a moment, then with a *fizzle* and *pop*, it disappeared.

"Too wet," he said shaking his head. Ember wriggled up from below, she could help with that.

Using her tail Ember bound Snitch's wet hands, together. Her scales started to glow a fiery red and steam began to rise until Snitch's gloves were completely dry.

This time they worked and with a loud *CLAP* Snitch's keyboard sparked into life. He tapped away studying the information scrolling across his glasses, reviewing all Maisie's bad dreams.

"Wow Maisie you have had some adventures with us, and yes, it does appear you are afraid of just about everything, a bit like me" he sniffed

31

pushing his slipping glasses back up his wet nose. "It could be one of many things inside."

His glasses crackled into life shooting out several beams of light towards the closed door. As an image of the room beyond appeared Snitch started to look for anything that could be lurking inside.

"See anything?" asked Noggin.

"Oh yes I see something" replied Snitch "but not very clearly, it's just a shape, but it's huge. I think it could be a m……."

"Well, there is only one way to find out" interrupted Maisie as she was cold and wet and wanted to get home. Maisie grabbed the door handle impatiently and flung it open.

"…onster" finished Snitch.

The giant hairy beast with its glowing eyes, clawed fingers, and brown rotting teeth ran across the room sending desks flying as it snarled wildly.

"DOOR MAISIE" yelled Fitz as she slammed it in the monster's face.

The monster crashed into the door glass with a *THUMP*, and they watched its squashed face slide down the glass leaving a slimy trail of green monster snot and slobber on the glass.

"*Pheweey*" exclaimed Noggin "that monster has worse breath than the one in our friend Jack's nightmare. Ugh boiled cabbage, old fish and rotten eggs," she said holding her nose.

"I'm not sure it's bad breath" replied Fitz as a green haze started to appear behind the glass and seep out under the door.

"Oh, my I think I'm going to faint" whimpered a very pale Snitch as the light went out in the monster's room.

"Only one left," whispered Maisie.

CHAPTER 3

Tickle

Maisie climbed over the moving vines that were now so dense she could no longer see any of the black and white floor tiles.

The air was much cooler at this end of the corridor and the jungle darker with thick leaves and vegetation blocking out the view of the corridor they left behind.

The only light remaining came from beyond the frosted glass of the last door. Even that was not as bright as the other rooms, it was so dim you could hardly see anything in its red glow.

"Are you sure about this" gulped Snitch.

Maisie started to shiver from being wet and cold. "It's the last one, it could be the way out," she said hopefully turning the door handle and cautiously opening the door.

Under the dim light they could just make out the room identical to the others, but this time on the opposite wall was another door, open with just a sliver of sunlight creeping in.

"The way out," cried a delighted Maisie "look I told you" as she started to hurry into the room.

"MAISIE, STOP WAIT" cried Noggin from her shoulder, "you don't know what's in there."

At first, it felt like a tickle or maybe a piece of fluff, that landed on Maisie's face in the dim light. She wiped it away with her fingers, then another and another. Something was dangling in front of her like thin cotton threads floating in the air.

"This does not look good," said Fitz to Noggin rubbing the sticky threads from his face.

More appeared the further they walked across the room, sticking and tangling them until Maisie stopped in her tracks.

"I can't move" she cried "I'm stuck in something."

The more she wiggled the more she became stuck and her feet were no longer on the floor. In the low red light, there was a sound like scuttling of tiny feet, lots of feet. Maisie froze in terror.

"Err, Maisie that thing you're most scared of, the thing you cannot say, it wouldn't happen to spin webs would it?" asked Noggin looking upwards. Maisie nodded slowly.

"I thought it might" replied Noggin tapping Fitz on the shoulder and pointing to the ceiling.

There above hung a gigantic spider, with long spindly legs, lots of black beady eyes and big fangs nipping together.

"Oh, great spiders" squealed Snitch, "I think I preferred the two headed shark" as he dropped back inside the pocket to hide.

"Spiders-spiders-spiders" whispered petrified Maisie over and over puffing faster and faster.

The spider slowly dropped on a thin line, coming to investigate the tasty treat trapped in its web. The closer the spider got the more Maisie wiggled and the more she wiggled the more she stuck. Fitz and Noggin were holding on with all their might to the wriggling terrified Maisie.

"FITZ DO YOUR THING BEFORE WE BECOME A SPIDERS DINNER" screamed Noggin.

"AND HURRY UP" yelled Snitch from below.

Dropping into the dressing gown hood Fitz slipped off his backpack. With care, he reached inside and lifted out a small white Dream Catcher Pearl before he clambered back up to Maisie's shoulder and stood trying hard to keep his balance.

"Maisie you have to stay still right now and trust us, remember it's a dream, *a dream*," said Noggin holding on tight.

Maisie froze as the giant spider stopped with its face was almost touching hers. Each of its eyes shone with a reflection of her face, and its fangs snapped together dripping with drool. Drawing in a deep breath Maisie's scream was ear shattering as she closed her eyes.

An almighty blast of icy wind exploded in the air, followed by a loud sucking and slurping noise. The blast propelled the startled spider away for a moment before it swung back like a pendulum at speed. As it swung across the room a whirlpool of air surrounding them began to suck everything into the tiny pearl Fitz was grasping tightly in his hands.

The giant spider, the desks and the webs, the corridor, the jungle, the wolf, the shark, the monster and monkeys, the glass frogs, all the creepy crawlies and every one of the doors were being pulled in like a giant spinning tornado.

Eyes screwed shut Maisie squealed as her hair thrashed around in the swirling freezing air whipping her in the face.

Silence…

With a bump Fitz, Noggin, Snitch, and Ember landed on Maisie's soft covers. They were crumpled and hanging at a funny angle from all the wriggling in her sleep.

Henry the tabby cat lay on the bottom of the bed and was not pleased with being woken by them as he had so many times before. He looked at them with one green eye and then drifted back to sleep in his comfortable spot.

Maisie was sound asleep in her messy bed with her head partly buried under the covers and her toy unicorn just peeping out. Neatly folded on a chair lay her new uniform, shoes, and rucksack ready for her first day of school.

"Aha" whispered Snitch, "the first day of school nightmare, that explains a lot."

"Always a scary time" replied Noggin.

"She will be fine," said Fitz in a hushed voice as he opened his backpack again carefully so as not to damage the cargo inside.

Nestled inside were two pearls. One was a Dream Catcher Pearl now black as night and churning with the nightmare trapped inside, and another, even smaller pearl, that was golden and shimmered with rainbow colours as he lifted it out.

"I do love this bit" whispered Snitch as Fitz crept past the sleeping Maisie so not to disturb her. Disappearing for a moment under the corner of her pillow he returned without the tiny pearl, which he left slightly cracked open, safely underneath.

"There, one Dream Pearl delivered safe and sound. I hope it's a fun dream Maisie," he said.

"Sweet dreams and enjoy school tomorrow" whispered Noggin.

Maisie sighed as she settled down to her delivered dream of riding on a beautiful golden unicorn through woods and streams like a princess.

She would not remember the monkeys, the wolf, the two headed shark, the monster, the spiders, or any of the nightmare they just shared....

She would not remember the three tiny people on their faithful red dragon…. but then again… she never did.

"Well, no windows open tonight," said Fitz as the three clambered aboard Ember.

"I guess we will be using Henry's door then" smiled Noggin as Henry opened an eye at the mention of his name.

With the three Dream Drifters safely aboard Ember flew down the stairs in the stillness of the night, along the hall and into the kitchen. On the worktop, stood a large chocolate cake covered in gooey chocolate icing, and on the top was **'FIRST DAY OF SCHOOL'** written in pink with a small plastic unicorn standing proudly in the middle.

"Oh, Ember please no one will know" promised Noggin.

Ember flew across the kitchen and low over the cake. The cheeky trio reached down a finger each dragging them through the sweet chocolatey icing.

"Yummy," said Snitch licking his finger clean. "Maybe we can come back tomorrow and have a whole piece."

Henry's cat flap popped open with a push and Ember flew out into the cool blustery night air.

"Time for home Ember as quick as you can," said Fitz. "There is a lot of ghastly nightmares rolled into one in this pearl and I want to get it locked safely away in the Night Warriors vault as soon as possible."

Embers scales started to glow red and orange warming the Dream Drifters like a dragon radiator beneath them. With a swoop of her immense wings, they set off into the night air beyond the clouds heading home to Dolomite Dell.

43

CHAPTER 4

Wind Woozels

The bitter night air stung their cheeks, as they flew homeward bound. Below clusters of town and village lights twinkled in the darkness as car lights moved on invisible roads between them. The lights got smaller and smaller as Ember climbed until they became just pinpricks on a map of darkness below.

Flying through a thick cloud they came out of the top and were surprised to find themselves surrounded by a large herd of grazing Wind Woozels. Their large trumpet shaped mouths stuck through the clouds as they blew a strong blustery wind to the earth below.

"*Brrrr,* no wonder its windy tonight" shivered Snitch "there are Wind Woozels everywhere."

Each passing cloud was covered in these curious four legged, shaggy creatures that, along with the Dream Drifters, call the floating island in the stars home.

With their warm rainbow coloured hair, trumpet shaped mouths, long floppy ears, hooved feet, and tails that resemble kites blowing in the wind, they are a remarkable sight.

Above the Woozel clouds, the sky became illuminated by a million stars and the moon glowed a frosty white. Embers strong wings beat hard as she rushed through the night, she wanted to get home to her warm bed just as much as the team of Dream Drifters on her back.

45

"Ahoy" came the cry from below. Rising from the clouds appeared a sleek white dragon with piercing blue eyes and a pale blue shimmer to her scales from the reflecting moonlight. Her name was Moonstone and upon her back rode her team Linc, Nift and Sneak

"Ahoy" called back Fitz "busy night?"

"Well it's sure a windy one, I think every Wind Woozel from home is out here and when isn't it a busy night?" called back Linc, the other team's leader. "One boogeyman from under William's bed captured and locked away" as he patted his backpack.

"Are you sure he's locked away, your backpacks jumping around a bit?" questioned Snitch as it bounced up and down.

"Ha, ha no he got hiccups with fright when Linc opened the pearl and he's still got them" chuckled back Nift. "I think he's new at this as he went a bit of a funny colour, so I hope he's not been sick in there or Bysidian and his team will not be happy when they go inside."

"Oh, the glamorous life of a Night Warrior battling nightmares in boogeyman sick" smiled Noggin as they all laughed. "Have you seen anyone else tonight?"

"Knip and her team Noodle and Whiz were here, you must have just missed them. We bumped into them as we left William's house, I think they came from the house next door. It was a bit strange though, they did not seem very happy and were covered in red shiny marks."

Fitz laughed, "the house next door, that's Jasper's house and you know what he has nightmares about?" he said looking back at Snitch.

Snitch beamed a huge grin "Oh yes I sure do, red shiny lipstick sounds like the giant Kissing Granny again to me."

"*Yuck*, do you remember her?" Noggin cried, "all she did was try to kiss you with her big wrinkly lips covered in thick ref lipstick and dribble. Her false teeth would click and clack as she sucked them, and she smelt of lavender water" she shuddered. "I thought we caught her though?"

"We did?" replied Fitz "Bysidian and his team went in to fight her but escaped as fast as they could, don't you remember them falling out into the Nightmare Vault covered in lipstick and granny slobber? She must have escaped."

"Or they set her free" laughed Snitch at the memory.

"Ah yes, I remember now, and didn't Quillion Quartz say he would feed you to their dragons if you told anyone?" reminded Noggin.

"Ah yes, yes he did, good point" replied Fitz "probably best to keep that a secret."

"I have an idea, how about a race?" suggested Noggin. "We're all heading home as dawn is coming soon and it will make the journey so much more fun."

"Oh, Noggin no please," said Snitch, but before he could finish his wailing Moonstone shot out in front of them.

"See you at home slow coaches" called Sneak as they disappeared into the clouds before Noggin could even blink.

"WHAT ARE WE WAITING FOR? LET'S GO EMBER" she cried. Every so often they caught a glimpse of the white dragon darting in and out of view when all of a sudden there loomed an enormous black cloud in the distance.

"I don't like the look of that one," called Snitch hanging on the back with all his strength. 'It's almost as if it has a face staring at us."

"No look and neither do they" called Fitz as Moonstone and her team turned and flew around it.

"Now's our chance" cried Noggin never wanting to lose. "Go through girl it's the only way to get in front."

Ember slowed a little, something didn't feel right, why had Moonstone gone around?

"Come on Ember what are you waiting for?" hollered Noggin as they disappeared into the blackness.

Like a thick fog, the cloud engulfed them in cold wet air as Ember battled through.

"Can anybody see anything?" called Snitch "my glasses are completely misted up."

"No nothing, just hold on tight and Ember get us out of here as fast as you can something doesn't feel right" ordered Fitz.

The steel net landed on them from nowhere as Ember stopped in mid-air and bundled into a twisting turning pile with Fitz, Noggin, and Snitch trapped inside her wings.

"Noggin, Snitch?" gasped Fitz as he was crushed against the dragon's body.

"I lost my glasses" cried Snitch in terror I can hardly see anything. What's happening?"

"I'm here, I'm ok" called back Noggin desperately trying to reach her belt and help Ember.

The net started to lift slowly through the cloud when a shape came into sight above, a long black shadow shaped like a boat hull with voices coming from it.

"Heave away lads, come on heave. The captains going to be mighty pleased with us, I can't believe we caught one"

"Oh no, pirates" whispered Fitz.

Higher and higher they climbed until they swung face to face with the cannons. Ember began to struggle but it was hopeless, she couldn't move, and she could feel the three Dream Drifters being crushed against her body.

The net reached the ship's deck as the thick cloud cleared revealing 'The Swirling Pearl' in all her evil glory. Pirates ran everywhere preparing for their prisoners as a team struggled to wind in the net's rope. Fed through a wooden arm hanging over the ship's side the net slowly reached the top and stopped swinging in mid-air.

"Watch it now lads, careful, we don't want to drop them. Not yet anyway" cried one with wonky eyes and a scruffy black beard as he held onto the wheel.

"Grab it Three-Toes, there, grab that piece of wood and jam it in here" he bellowed as another jammed a long piece of wood in the wheel to stop it turning.

"Fitz, what's happening?" whimpered Snitch from below Ember "I'm scared I can't see."

Noggins voice called from above. "It's alright Snitch, we're all together and nothing's going to happen to you, I promise," she lied tried to hide the fear in her voice.

"Quick fetch the captain, tell him we have a little present for him" a pirate shouted from the deck as another ran off in the direction of the captain's quarters.

"Right lads swing them in so he can see them properly."

"Heave", a team of pirates ran to the wooden arm and pushed with all their might until the net swung around and came to a halt above the deck.

"HOLD ON" one shouted, "Well I don't believe my eyes, look Boz-Eye it's them, it's them from the Tower in London."

"No, it can't be" replied Boz-Eyed Bert walking forward to see better. "You're right it is, well blow me down with a seagulls trump. Leave us hanging there to be caught, would you? Kick me in the shins, would you? Well, you're going to get it now" he smirked through black rotting teeth.

TAP, TAP, TAP the wooden deck shook as the pirates parted. Captain Solomon Fear stood before them with his rugged face covered in scars and one evil eye covered with a leather patch. His long black hair was swept back with a piece of tattered old snakeskin and through an unruly stubble beard gleamed one golden tooth.

"Get them down quickly you fool" he shouted, "we need to cover that dragon's eyes, or we'll be surrounded by Night Warriors before you know it."

With that Three-Toes Magee ran and grabbed the wooden stick locking the wheel.

"Hold on" cried Fitz as they dropped through the air landing with an almighty smash on the deck.

"Ember, Ember are you alright?" cried Noggin as Ember groaned in pain.

"Oh, stop worrying little missy, nothings broken, not yet anyway" the captain sniggered.

"Let us out of here and I'll show what can be broken" stormed Noggin.

"*OOOOHHH*, we're so scared" came the chorus from the pirates as they laughed loudly.

"Bysidian and his men will be here any moment then you won't be so brave," said Fitz.

"Now how do you think they will find you?" asked Solomon Fear walking to the net and leaning close to Fitz's face. "All they saw was you flying into a large cloud, and yes, I am sure they can see us on my glorious ship through your dragon's eyes, but we could be anywhere. Besides they are about to lose sight of you all together."

With that, he pulled the silver serpent top off his cane. A cloud of fine dust lifted into the air and with a blow from his flaking cracked lips, it engulfed the net, and everyone trapped inside.

"Night, night enjoy your sleep" he whispered into Fitz's ear as everything went black.

CHAPTER 5

Fire

There was a flicker of light as Ember managed to open one eye slightly. Again, and again she tried but they felt so heavy, and her head felt woozy. The last thing she remembered was Solomon Fear standing over them and then nothing.

Solomon Fear, yes that was it she remembered, Pirates, Fitz, Noggin, and Snitch, where were they? She opened her eyes to find herself once again dangling above the ship trapped inside the net.

Below on deck, all the pirates had gathered around, what was happening?

Then she saw them, the three tiny Dream Drifters stood at the end of the plank with their hands tied. Snitch was shaking in fear blind without his glasses, Fitz was standing in front trying to protect him whilst holding Noggin back who was lunging wildly at the pirate captain stood before them.

"Boss, Boss the dragons waking up, you'd better hurry she doesn't look very happy."

Solomon Fear looked up and at that very moment, Ember's head cleared from the sleep dust. With a roar of anger, she blew with all her power a rush of molten fire and slowly the steel net surrounding her started to melt.

"She's breaking out. RUN, RUN" came the cries from the not so brave pirates as they dodged and dived to avoid the falling hot sparks and dripping liquid metal. "FIRE, FIRE" they screamed as the wooden deck started to burn before the flames fizzled out in the moist cold air.

"Now the question is," said Solomon Fear to Fitz calmly "what will she do? She has two choices either stop us or save *YOU*" he screeched as he drew his sword and rushed towards them.

As the three disappeared off the end of the plank Ember used all her anger to burst free from the melting net.

Down through the dense black cloud, down, down, down where were they she couldn't see them. Then somewhere below her, she heard Snitch screaming at the top of his lungs.

"AAAAARRRGGGHHHH"

Ember exploded out of the bottom of the cloud, she could see.

One, two, three falling Dream Drifters came into view and folding her wings back she dropped like an arrow catching Snitch first, followed by Fitz in

59

her talons. Noggin was further below, and the lights of the village were getting closer and closer. Without a second to lose Ember darted after Noggin who was frantically trying to untie her hands.

"*EMBER*" she yelled as she saw Maisie's garden rushing towards her and the large tree she was about to crash into. Stretching her tied hands above her, she closed her eyes in hope as Ember hooked her fang through the knotted rope just as they crashed through the treetop. Bouncing off branches *THUMP-THUMP-THUMP,* down towards the ground until they landed with a hard *THUD* on the grass below.

Henry the cat looked at the dragon and little people bundle on the floor in utter disgust before walking away and returning to the warmth of Maisie's bed.

Every part of Ember ached as she rose to her feet looking at Snitch, Noggin, and Fitz to check they were unhurt. In turn, she blew a spark at each pair of bound hands and the ropes frazzled and snapped. All three were in one piece, cut and bruised with leaves and branches jammed in their hair and clothes but they were alive. Snitch was softly sobbing afraid and unable to see clearly without his lost glasses when there came a shout.

"My belt, they took my belt and everything on it" screamed Noggin.

"That's not all they took," groaned Fitz getting to his feet. "My backpack's gone."

61

CHAPTER 6

Home

"Here, over here I've found them."

In a flash of wings and flap of his black cloak the Night Warrior, Templar Storm landed beside them aboard his majestic dragon Ammolite. Swiftly following were Lucius Squall and Fabian Feldspar in their black armour, swords gleaming, astride their dragons Heliodor and Nebular.

"Are you all alright, we have been searching for you everywhere?" asked Lucius as he slid from his saddle and ran to help them.

"The Guardians lost sight of you when you entered that cloud, what were you thinking? We had no way of tracking you and then the next thing we knew you were surrounded by pirates," said Fabian helping Snitch to his feet. "As soon as we saw you were in trouble Bysidian sent us to help but we only found you when Ember broke through the cloud as you fell."

"What happened up there?" asked Templar as he tended to Ember's cuts and scrapes.

"They took my backpack and the Nightmare Pearl," said Fitz "and Noggins belt of gadgets."

"And they made me lose my glasses" wailed Snitch "I'm helpless without them."

"No Snitch you are *never* helpless, *never* say that. We are a team remember?" said Noggin angrily walking out from under the tree and looking towards the clouds. "They are still up there, they can't have gone far and there are six of us now and four dragons," she said looking at the three Night Warriors standing before her. "I have no idea why

63

he wants that pearl and my gadgets, but you can bet it's for something wicked. I don't know about you, but I say we get them back."

"THERE, LOOK" yelled Fitz. In the distance way above the pirate ship caught the moonlight as it broke from the cover of one cloud to move to another.

"Leave this to us," said Templar as the three Night Warriors rushed to their dragons. "We can handle Solomon Fear, we don't want you getting hurt anymore."

"NO WAY, we are coming like it or not" snapped Fitz. "He has no right to do this to my team," he said helping Snitch to his seat, "and we can help."

"LET'S GO" cried Noggin launching herself into the saddle and hanging onto Ember who was pouring smoke from her nose as fury glinted in her green eyes.

"Then you had better keep up and stay behind us at all times do you understand?" shouted Templar Storm as Ammolite rose into the air.

Higher and higher they flew into the night heading towards where they had last seen 'The Swirling Pearl.' Scattered breaks in the clouds allowed the moon to shine through lighting their way as they darted between Wind Woozels covered clouds, all the time going up and up.

"Where are you, where are you?" whispered Fitz to himself looking around.

"THERE" cried Lucius as the pirate ship sailed into view way in the distance. Her tattered sails flapped in the wind and the sound of Solomon Fear bellowing orders to his crew drifted in the air.

"They are moving so fast" cried Noggin, all these Wind Woozels are filling the sails for them.

Higher and higher they went, the four dragons were flying at speed, but the wind was so strong they could not catch up.

"Stay with him" called Fabian "don't lose sight of that ship or we will never get close to them. Use the clouds as a cover so they can't see us coming."

"Where are they going?" called Fitz "they don't look like they plan to land soon and surely there is nothing out here" he questioned looking lost around the night sky.

Snitch had been quiet in his seat until now, watching a blurred shape in the distance come and go between clouds and trying to think what it could be. Larger and larger the shape became clearer and clearer.

"Home" he whispered.

"What did you say, I can't hear you?" called Noggin straining her eyes looking for the hidden ship.

"HOME, HOME" yelled Snitch "LOOK."

As the clouds cleared, floating before them shone the island they called home drifting on its cloud sea and heading directly for it was 'The Swirling Pearl.'

****

Deep inside Dreamcast Mountain the leader of the Night Warriors, Bysidian Black and his remaining man, Quillion Quartz, had been watching everything through Ember's eyes in a large crystal ball. Pacing impatiently back and forth his black boots echoed on the stone floor. He was desperate to help, but they could not leave the island and the vaults unprotected.

Stood beside them was the High Minister, leader of the Guardians watching silently, his long white robes swayed against his walking stick and his worried eyes framed by his long white hair and beard.

All of a sudden, the clouds blocking Ember's view parted and they saw their island home with the ship heading straight towards them.

"They're not going to catch that ship in time," said Quillion. "They're too far behind Bysidian" as he ran from the room into the maze of mountain corridors.

"The vaults, they're coming for the vaults and the pearls High Minister. Gather your Guardians and get them to a safe place as quickly as you can, we have no time to lose" instructed Bysidian Black as he ran from the room.

Down the lamp lit passageways, they ran opening every door and warning anyone within of the impending attack. As word spread the corridors started to fill with white robed Guardians and teams of tiny Dream Drifters dashing for cover.

"But they were right behind us, I just thought they had come home and left for the night in a huff after they lost the race" cried Linc.

"Pirates, I can't believe we missed them, it could have been us" cried Sneak. "Poor Snitch he must be terrified."

"We have to get out of the mountain," said Nift as they stopped at the large dark opening of a tunnel slide. "We have to climb up and get out of here, back to Cloud Bay and Dolomite Dell to warn everyone outside."

Leaving the commotion behind, they began the steep climb up the slippery slide into the blackness beyond.

****

Bysidian and Quillion had reached the circular iron door protecting the Granite Vault with its

69

engraved dragon wings flickering in the lamplight. Inside row upon row of Dream Pearls, each partnered with a Dream Catcher Pearl created by the Guardians for the Dream Drifter teams to use on their nightly missions.

As the giant round door swung open the golden light within shone out reflecting on their armour and swords.

"Stand guard here" ordered Bysidian as he grabbed a nearby lantern and ran inside. Across the vault away from the golden light, the air turned bitterly cold and black as night, the wind howled and Bysidian's cloak flapped wildly.

Further and further he ran until in his lanterns glow another door appeared, thick and iron like the Granite Vault's only this one displayed a screaming face of terror.

Placing the flickering lantern on the floor Bysidian hauled the door open with a violent gust of wind, just enough to look inside.

Within the air was so cold he could see his breath and the entire room moaned and wailed with the storm that was trapped inside. Taking a small purple crystal from his armour he threw it into the vault, it rose into the air higher and higher until finally, it disappeared. After a moment from somewhere overhead, a purple glow appeared falling like purple rain until the entire room was bathed in its dim light.

Lining the walls were row upon row of pearls, black as night and shrouded in a hazy fog from the damp cold air. Bysidian watched as the pearls turn blacker and blacker with every deafening moan and wail. The churning fog became thicker by the second and the pearls began to shiver as if they were alive and trying to escape.

"They can feel him coming" he whispered as each hair on his neck stood on end, "every one of those imprisoned nightmares can feel Solomon Fear and his evil coming."

With a heave Bysidian slammed the vault door shut and, making sure it was firmly locked, he ran back to Quillion who was standing guard as instructed.

"He's close they can feel him I've never seen or heard anything like it before," said Bysidian "It's as if they are calling him to release them."

With swords drawn the two heroic Night Warriors closed the Granite Vault door locking the Dream Catcher and Nightmare Pearls within, ready to defend them with their lives.

CHAPTER 7

Fog Flompers

Flying against the howling wind the dragons battled on when from nowhere dancing sparks of light appeared filling the air around them.

"The Dew Dancers returning home" called Noggin as one whizzed past here ear still glistening from scattering their dew on the Earth overnight.

As the sparkling sprites caught up with the pirate ship they seemed to slow in fear before circling it curiously and whizzing away, disappearing to the island beyond.

"They have to warn everyone, they have to."

"No one will listen," said Snitch "you know they are too naughty. Everyone will think they are just playing another silly trick."

"Bysidian will know" called Templar Storm. "He'll have seen through Embers eyes, he and Quillion will be prepared, or at least I hope they are as they're the only protection everyone has right now."

As he spoke the pirate ship was engulfed by the island clouds and vanished.

The three Night Warrior dragons stopped mid-flight leaving Ember to zoom past.

"What are you doing, why are you stopping?" cried Noggin with angry tears in her eyes as Ember turned.

"We can't just fly in, they could be waiting for us just beyond the clouds" answered Lucius Squall. "If we get caught Bysidian and Quillion are alone against the whole ship full of pirates. We need another way in."

"Oh, I'm so useless without my glasses" wailed Snitch "I can't look for anything."

"Don't worry Snitch, Ember and I might just know a way" replied Fitz. "Follow us."

The four dragons plunged beneath the island's clouds, dropping until they arrived at the bottom of the island. Shrouded in clouds were tall rugged rock faces pointing down to Earth way below.

"How do you know about this place?" asked Noggin looking around in the mist confused.

"Training" replied Fitz. "When you are trained as a leader and assigned a Dream Dragon one of the first things, we have to do is learn everywhere on the island above and below. It's how I bonded with Ember and how we became a team."

75

"Could someone *please* explain where we are?" asked a fed up Snitch.

"Underneath the island Snitch" replied Noggin. "There are rockfaces hidden in the clouds like a gigantic mountain but hanging upside down with some caves in them."

"Oh, the Fog Flompers caves, *of course,* good thinking Fitz" replied Snitch.

"Hang on a second, you knew about these?" snapped Noggin.

"Of course I did silly, I didn't learn how to become a Knowledge Keeper without at least knowing all about our island, honestly it's basic training silly. Don't tell me you didn't know they were here?" he joked. "Next thing you'll tell us is that you have never heard of the Ice Imps, Frost Fairies and Hail Hurlers that live in the snow on the top of the mountain."

"Oh, that's a bad move she's going to blow" whispered Fitz as Noggin's face grew redder and redder.

"If it's any help Noggin we didn't know they existed either," said Fabian Felspar "but then again we don't tend to come out of Dreamcast Mountain that often."

"Well they look like a good way inside to me," said Lucius looking at the nearest cave "follow me" as Heliodor shot inside.

"No, not that one it's this way" called Fitz pointing as Lucius disappeared from view.

"Why, what's in that one?" asked Templar Storm looking concerned.

"I don't know, I've never been inside that one, have you Ember?" replied Fitz as Ember shook her head.

From the distance and gradually getting louder came a ringing noise of lots of little bells. Louder and louder

BBBBRRRRIIIIINNNGGGG!!!

now why does that sound familiar?" asked Fitz.

Like a bullet from a gun, Heliodor flew out of the cave surrounded by dozens of small flying alarm clocks.

"Aha, so *that's* where they all go" laughed Fitz as they flew away into the night sky ringing in disgust at being disturbed. "At least half of those must be mine."

Noggin and Snitch tried to hide their giggles as a flustered Lucius flew back to their side.

"Well that way won't work" he coughed trying to hide his embarrassment as Templar and Fabian grinned. "After you, I think," he said with a wave of his hand towards Fitz and Ember.

"Do you think they heard that?" asked Snitch. "They must have heard the bells."

"Well if the pirates didn't the Fog Flompers sure did" replied Fitz pointing towards the large hairy creatures watching them from the shadows of the caves.

Ember flew into an opening as the large hairy Fog Flompers that had been watching stepped further back into the shadows.

As quietly as possible she landed followed by the three Night Warrior dragons.

"They won't hurt you" whispered Fitz "they are just incredibly shy and scared of strangers. Don't make too much noise and no fast movements. We don't want to alarm them."

"Why do they live down here in the dark?" asked Noggin in a hushed voice.

"They like the cool damp air" replied Snitch "it helps them make the fog.

"Make the fog?" questioned Noggin confused.

"Yes, where on earth do you think fog comes from?" asked Snitch.

"I always thought it was when the air turned colder, and the water vapour condenses into tiny water droplets that are suspended in the air" replied Noggin.

With that Snitch started to laugh so it echoed loudly around them. "Honestly Noggin you do have some funny ideas" he cried wiping tears of laughter from his eyes.

Slowly one of the hairy creatures moved from the shadows to examine their uninvited visitors. It was big and round covered head to foot in long brown shaggy hair and on its huge pink hairy feet and hands were yellow nails. It had a large plump pink nose and a ginormous mouth along with the kindest eyes Noggin had ever seen.

Gradually another appeared, then another and another not wishing the visitors any harm but wary and curious of them.

Keeping a safe distance from the dragons the hairy beasts plodded their way to the entrance of the cave and stopped. As night had fallen on the island it meant morning was just breaking on Earth and they had a job to do.

"What are they doing?" asked Noggin watching in fascination.

The largest Fog Flomper began to hum, then another and another until the low humming sound vibrated around the cave. Gradually the sound spread until it came from every cave entrance scattered around the upside down mountains.

It wasn't a scary sound but calming and comforting when all of a sudden it stopped. With a deep breath in the Fog Flompers opened their vast gaping mouths and slowly breathed out.

A billowing white fog waterfall, damp and cool like the surrounding caves poured out of their mouths. It flowed from every cave down through the clouds and fell to Earth.

"That will please the people down there" said Fitz "they don't seem to like the fog for some reason."

Little by little the fog stopped as the hairy creatures ran out of breath and their mouths closed. Then as quietly as they appeared, they disappeared into the shadows.

"They are amazing," said Noggin with a smile.

"Well you learn something new every day," said Fabian looking at his fellow Night Warriors.

"They know we mean no harm, we're safe to travel through their caves now," said Fitz as Ember took off. "This way, follow us."

****

Under cover of darkness a tip of mast rose from Cloud Bay. Another appeared, then another poking through the billowing cloud sea, each draped with tattered grey sails and covered with ropes.

Taller and taller until a figurehead of a dragon winged serpent appeared from the haze, its mouth stretched wide with silver fangs and orange eyes gleaming in the tiny streetlights as if keeping watch.

Rising from the clouds 'The Swirling Pearl' was as silent as could be. The pirates lined the deck not making a sound as Solomon Fear guided his ship towards the white sands of the beach.

Rows of tiny lights twinkled in the dark house lined streets and way into the leafy forest dell, everyone was inside unaware of the pirate's arrival.

The ship stopped and from behind the wheel, Solomon Fear looked out towards Dreamcast Mountain. His golden tooth twinkled in the moonlight as he grinned

"There she is boys" he whispered to his men. "That's where we need to be deep inside that mountain and at them vaults. Listen, you can almost hear the evil nightmares inside calling to us" cupping his hand to his ear.

"I can't hear a thing, can you? I must be going deaf," said the pirate they called Three-Toes Magee loudly.

"Shushhhh" hissed Boz-Eyed Bert standing next to him, "do you want to change your name to Two-Toes because you're going the right way about it" he warned as his right eye rolled the opposite direction to his left.

"Just saying that's all," said Three-Toes as he stretched his neck listening for the magical calling pearls the captain spoke of.

"Fetch the pearl" Solomon Fear ordered in a stern voice "but make sure it's safe we don't want it opening too soon."

****

"Hurry we're almost there" called back Nift to her teammates clambering up the slippery slide behind her.

"Finally," came the echoing voice of Sneak "my arms and legs are about to fall off" he moaned.

"Please still be there, please," said Linc as he clambered out of the slide and ran across the locker room to the door.

Waiting patiently on her landing bay was Moonstone, a little confused to see her three tiny teammates back so soon.

Linc heaved a sigh of relief "Pirates Moonstone, the pirates are coming, we have to get out of here and warn everyone on the island quickly," he said as he ran for her saddle followed by Nift and Sneak.

With a flash of leathery wings, the dazzling white dragon turned and flew towards the opening at the mountain top as fast as she could go.

CHAPTER 8

Codswallop

Without a sound, the menacing black ship rose from the cloud sea and into the air. The clouds clung to the sides as if trying to hold it back but fell away helplessly as it flew across the streets of tiny houses below.

"Quietly now lads, we don't need everyone to know we are here" he called in a hushed voice to the crew who were moving around the creaking ship tending to their duties.

"Of course, one person will know I'm here" he whispered to himself with a grin. "Be ready Bysidian as trouble is coming" he cackled.

"I don't get it" whispered Three-Toes Magee to Boz-Eye Bert "what about that Night Warrior army, won't they be in there? Because if they are, I certainly won't be racing inside."

"*Hush stupid*" replied Boz-Eye "why do you think the captain threw them, silly little Dream Drifters, overboard and didn't just keep them as prisoners?"

"Erm, to see if they could fly?" asked Three-Toes.

"Codswallop, honestly sometimes even you must be astounded by your own stupidity" huffed Boz-Eye in disbelief. "It was a decoy dummy, the Night Warriors would know they were in trouble and come out to help. Maybe not all of them but you can bet most of them came and that means less to fight in there," he said pointing at the approaching mountain.

"Aye, Magee, remember last time?' interrupted another pirate close by. "Captain waited until they were inside that Nightmare Pearl and only their leader was left. It didn't take old Sky-High Charlie here long to blow those vaults, did it?" he said patting the shoulder of a tall, boney, one armed pirate stood next to him with dynamite sticks dangling from his pockets. "He didn't stand a chance against us all then and he won't this time neither."

Higher and higher the ship rose into the air casting an ominous shadow across the tiny rooftops. As they flew above Dolomite Dell the thin wisps of smoke from the chimneys whipped and curled in the passing ships breeze.

Hidden in the undergrowth the Dew Dancers watched, their usual sparkling light only a faint glow so as not to be seen by the pirates above. They had tried to warn the Dream Drifters, but no one would listen. Being so small and naughty they simply batted them away as a nuisance like a fly. Maybe they would listen next time?

Herds of grazing Wind Woozels were drifting in on clouds, returning to the rugged grassy plains where they lived. Startled by the passing ship, they ran for cover in the craggy rocks around the base of Dreamcast Mountain and watched in fear as the ship rose up the mountainside to the ice and snow above.

The pirates shivered as they approached the glittering crystal homes of the Frost Fairies, Ice Imps, and Hail Hurlers. Their breath fogged in the freezing air and the grey ragged sails rippled in the icy breeze, showering the pirates with delicate crystals of ice.

All was quiet, the Frost Fairies and Ice Imps were on Earth travelling on the Fog Flompers fog to scatter their ice and frost on the human world below.

The Hail Hurlers were sound asleep snoring in their ice beds exhausted from a long night's work. Balls of manic blue fluff with big red noses and long stripy legs they were even more naughty than the Dew Dancer sprites. Travelling on immense thunderhead storm clouds they hurl frozen pellets of ice at anyone and anything that is unlucky enough to be in firing range.

Quietly the ship glided by their windows, unseen and unheard, any sound drowned out by their loud snoring.

"Just a little further, we're almost at the top lads"

****

91

Moonstone shot out the mountain top into the cold icy air with Linc, Nift and Sneak hanging on as tightly as they could.

"Where do we start?" called Nift to Linc looking at the island stretching out below.

"The Dell Moonstone, aim for Dolomite Dell as fast as you can, they can help spread the word to the people in Cloud Bay."

Moonstone flew down the mountainside through the ice-cold air freezing her wings tips when through a snowy haze the pirate ship appeared. Without a thought for her safety, camouflaged against the white of the snow, the sparkling dragon flew towards one of the grey sails. She burst straight through it ripping a large hole and disappeared into the wintry darkness below.

"Did you see that?" said Three-Toes Magee hanging onto a mast as the ship rocked from the impact.

"See what? I can't see anything" replied Boz-Eyed Bert as his eyes rolled around in different directions before one settled looking at his nose and the other straight up in the air.

"It was like a giant snowball hit us or something" continued Three-Toes looking around confused. Boz-Eye banged the side of his head with his hand and once his eyes were looking in the same direction he looked up. "Holy mackerel, that sails got a big hole in it, where did that come from?" he said.

"Don't know" replied Three-Toes "but look, if you squint it looks exactly like a dragon" he laughed.

The other pirates rallied around to drop the damaged sail when Solomon Fear bellowed, "we're here, steady as she goes." 'The Swirling Pearl' stopped directly above the deep dark hole which leads to the vaults and Guardians home way below.

****

The hairs on the back of Bysidian Blacks neck stood on end again "They're here," he said calmly to Quillion Quartz "be ready." With swords drawn the two Night Warriors held their breath listening and looking for any clue as to where the attack would come from.

A fast shuffling noise along the corridor made both turn and brandish their swords when the long white robes and frizzy white hair of one of the Guardians appeared.

"They're here, they're here" he called out waving his arms.

"Yes, the pirates are here, and you should be somewhere safe" replied Bysidian taking the Guardian's arm and trying to turn him around.

"No, no, no *they* are here, the others" the Guardian replied "Fitz's team and the other Night Warriors, they are inside the Fog Flompers caves right now and coming this way. The High Minister sent me to tell you. He's gone to open the door from here to the caves so they can get in."

"What caves and what on earth is a Fog Flomper? asked Quillion looking confused.

"Below, under the island, caves, big hairy creatures, bit smelly, not good at hygiene, you know? Oh, never mind,' replied the flustered Guardian scratching his curly beard. "He just wanted you to know helps on the way" he hollered as he turned and shuffled away.

Somewhere way above there echoed a loud *THUD* as 'The Swirling Pearl' dropped its anchor. The messenger Guardian stopped and looked at the two Night Warriors. "Pirates, oh my, good luck" he cried as he disappeared.

"Well if they are coming, they had better hurry," said Bysidian we need all the help we can get.

****

Floating above the mountain opening 'The Swirling Pearl' rocked to and fro heaving on her anchor as if trying to break free.

"STEADY, STEADY" yelled Solomon Fear to his men, his breath making a white fog in the bitter air as ice crystals formed on his beard. "MAKE WAY, LET HIM PASS." A shivering pirate carefully walked through the gathered crew carrying a small wooden chest so carefully it was as if his life depended on it.

Slowly Solomon Fear opened the lid and lifted out the black pearl inside. The air outside was freezing his fingers but still, the pearl felt even colder in his hands. He closed his eyes sensing the call of the nightmares within gaining power and wanting to be set free.

"Hush now my beauties" he whispered. "Your time has come, how dare they trap you inside this pearl prison. You want freedom and I need your help to get those pearls like you, locked in the vaults below. Together we are an army and they will never be able to stop us. With your help, I can set all the others free and we will be invincible" he cried holding the black pearl over the side of the ship.

"Who's he talking to?" whispered Three-Toes to Boz-Eye who shook his head in disbelief causing his eyes to jangle around.

"Oh, you'll see" replied the pirate they called Sky-High Charlie "this is where the fun really begins for all of us and my little friends here" as he patted the sticks of explosive poking out of his coat pocket.

97

"CATCH, BYSIDIAN BLACK" hollered Solomon Fear as he dropped it over the ship's side. With a thunderous *CRACK,* it hit the top of Dreamcast Mountain and smashed into a thousand pieces.

****

"NOOOOO" came the cry from Linc, Nift and Sneak as they watched the pearl drop. Like black billowing lava, the evil within exploded around the mountain top. Smoky black trails slithered down the mountainside disappearing onto the island below and as the large black storm of nightmares around the top dropped inside the mountain fell silent.

"What was in that pearl, did Fitz say?" asked Sneak trying to remember the conversation they had earlier that evening, it seemed a lifetime ago now.

"No, I don't think he did, Oh I can't remember" replied Nift "but you can bet its nothing good and it looked like more than one came out."

"We have to wake them up, we have to warn everyone NOW" instructed Linc.

Lights came on in the houses as the sound of the shattering pearl shook the island. Dream Drifters were running into the street, looking towards the mountain and the shadowy ship floating above it. Linc, Nift, and Sneak ran door to door banging to warn anyone they could find and as the message spread panic on the island started to rise.

Linc clambered onto Moonstones back and stood on the saddle. "EVERYONE LISTEN" he yelled loudly over the shouts of the terrified Dream Drifters. Slowly the shouting stopped, and they turned towards his voice. "You all have to go inside, lock your doors and windows tightly, close your curtains and block out the lights. Stay silent and do not come outside until one of us comes to tell you it's safe. Do not open your doors to anyone or anything else.

"*Anything* what do you mean *anything?*" came the cry from someone in the crowd.

"Some of the nightmares have spread onto the island, we don't know where or what they are yet" replied Nift. "The safest place for everyone is inside."

"But we can help" came the shout from other members of Dream Drifter teams as they moved forward through the crowds. "We capture nightmares every night, we must be able to do something?"

"What with?" called out Sneak. "We have no Dream Catcher Pearls, they are all in there" he pointed to the mountain. We were leaving for the night when they attacked. All of our pearls, gadgets, Seeker Glasses and gloves are inside, we have no help. We are not strong enough to fight the nightmares, that's the Night Warriors job, remember we only capture them."

"Bysidian Black and Quillion Quartz are inside as we speak protecting the vaults and the Guardians. We need to keep watch out here, do our best to protect Dolomite Dell, Cloud Bay, and everyone in them," said Linc trying to calm the situation.

"Where are the others?" someone shouted, "the other Night Warriors, why are there only two inside?"

"Don't panic they are on the way trust me, they had to leave the island on an emergency, but are almost back" lied Linc as he had no idea where they were.

As a team from Dolomite Dell hurried towards Cloud Bay to warn them of the danger and the streets began to empty, there came a rustling noise in the trees. A face appeared in the undergrowth and another and another. Brown and hairy with naughtiness in their eyes the trees started to fill with a gang of large swinging monkeys.

Screams of terror filled the streets. "INSIDE NOW" yelled Nift as doors slammed shut all around them and lights went out casting Dolomite Dell into darkness.

Aboard Moonstone they watched as the naughty monkeys spilt onto the streets chattering loudly, hanging on the streetlights, rattling the door knockers and trying to peep down the chimneys.

"Fitz, I don't know where you all are, but please hurry," said Linc as they flew towards Cloud Bay. Turning the rusty key to unlock the heavy wooden door the High Minister stepped back. Slowly it swung open with a loud creak, revealing a narrow stone tunnel leading down into darkness. Standing before him were Fitz, Noggin, Snitch and the three Night Warriors sent to rescue them.

"Oh, thank heavens you're all safe, quickly there is no time to lose," he said as he stepped aside allowing them to run past and up the steep stone staircase behind.

"Wait" called Templar Storm as he ran back into the caves to where the dragons waited. It was too narrow for them to follow and they would be no help in the tight maze of rooms and passageways inside.

"Ember, Heliodor, Nebular, Ammolite head back through the caves and get to the island outside. Make sure everyone is safe and help where you can but be ready, we'll need you when we call."

With a nod and a cloud of cave dust, they disappeared down the network of tunnels and back to the island above.

Up the stone staircase, round and round they ran. "Bysidian and Quillion, where are they High Minister?" called back Lucius to the white robed figure struggling to keep up on the stairs.

"The vaults, they're guarding the vaults" puffed the High Minister as he stopped and waved them to continue without him.

"They don't know, THEY DON'T KNOW HE HAS A NIGHTMARE PEARL" yelled Snitch hanging onto Noggin's arm to guide him.

Without warning, there was a ground shaking *CRACK* from somewhere way above followed by a loud ear piercing scream. As the ground shook dust and pieces of stone started to fall from the tunnel walls. Templar, Lucius, and Fabian each grabbed a Dream Drifter pulling them close under their capes and armour to protect them.

"WHAT'S THAT?" screamed Snitch closing his eyes tightly and putting his hands over his ears.

"*AAAAAAARRRRRGGGGHHHH* the mountains collapsing, we're all going to be buried" cried Noggin.

As suddenly as it started the rumbling stopped and silence fell leaving only dust falling in the staircase.

"No Noggin the mountains not collapsing" coughed Templar as he brushed the dust from his armour and sent Fabian back to make sure the High Minister was unhurt. "That was the sound of your stolen Nightmare Pearl being split open."

"The nightmares inside the mountain," gasped the out of breath High Minister as he appeared on the stairs. "You have to hurry."

Fitz looked at Noggin and then Snitch seeing the terror growing in their eyes. "High Minister there is more than one."

****

The orange glowing eyes came closer and closer through the fog, followed by a row of sharp white teeth. The giant wolf approached them along the corridor.

"Oh no please not another wolf," said Quillion standing his ground, sword raised. "If I had money for every time someone had a nightmare about a wolf, I would be a rich man. Is it just me though or did seem like an incredibly loud crack just for a trapped wolf?"

"Behind it, look they are using it as a shield" whispered Bysidian as row upon row of black boots gathered in the mist. Suddenly the wolf stopped, not to close, but close enough that the two Night Warriors could feel its warm breath wafting towards them.

From between the beast's front legs a figure appeared, Solomon Fear stood defiantly with his sword in hand.

"Look, look there's only two of them" came the cry from behind. "They won't be able to stop us all, they don't stand a chance" as the corridor erupted with hoots of laughter.

"QUIET" yelled Solomon Fear banging his sword on the floor. "Well, well, look who we have here, the formidable Bysidian Black and Quillion Quartz, it's an honour," he said with a bow and a sweep of his hat.

"Oh no, the honour will be all ours when you and your men are behind lock and key" replied Bysidian taking a step forward to block their path to the vault.

Solomon Fear shook his head slowly, "will you never learn? Do you think *two* of you can stop me and my army, including my new friend here?" as the wolf snarled. "But of course, I don't just have one new friend, oh no I have lots thanks to a full Nightmare Pearl from that useless team of Dream Drifters. Now you see, my new friends are not very happy with you, they didn't like being trapped inside that teeny tiny pearl unable to do what they love best."

A mixture of cackles and sniggers came from behind "Yeah, terrifying people they like that, they are not happy with you," hollered the pirates.

BANG! Solomon Fears sword hit the ground again hard and silence fell.

"Now move aside, we all know why we are here and what I want. Inside that vault is a whole army of nightmares waiting to be unleashed, I am not greedy, I don't want them all, just a few special ones. With their help I can steal all the treasure I desire from those people on Earth. I will be the richest pirate ever known."

With that, the whole corridor erupted into cheers and whoops from the pirate crew. Overhead on the pitch black ceiling, there was movement, slowly creeping along as the two Night Warriors were distracted. Without a sound the dark creeping shadow stopped above them and hung upside down, not seen or heard by anyone but the despicable pirate captain himself.

"We know exactly why you are here, and we know exactly what you want, but not one of those black pearls will be leaving the vault, not tonight or any other night" replied Bysidian boldly.

Solomon Fear laughed "Oh really, well who's going to stop us, two measly Night Warriors?"

"MAKE THAT FIVE" Templar Storm shouted as he and the other Night Warriors appeared from the shadows behind the pirate crew.

CHAPTER 9

The Last Dragon

"Oh boy, we're going to be in big trouble" moaned Three-Toes Magee as he scurried along the maze of corridors after Boz-Eyed Bert. "Tell me again why we had to take that tunnel slide and not one the others were using?" he asked.

"Because silly it was the fastest tunnel down here, none of the others knew what they were doing and it had nothing, absolutely nothing to do with the fact I slipped off the rope when we jumped from the ship and fell down it."

"Ah, I see" replied Three-Toes nodding. "But if it was the fastest slide why are we lost following this big hairy stinky monster through these passages and not with the others at the vault?"

"Tactics silly" replied Boz-Eye "We're bringing up the rear and making sure it's all safe whilst the others get the pearls."

"Well, we are bringing up somethings rear" replied Three-Toes as the monsters hairy behind waddled down the corridor before them. "Besides that, why do you get to wear that big belt thing with all those fancy thingamabobs on it, why can't I have a go?"

Suddenly the monster stopped next to a closed door and turned its head as if listening for something. *WALLOP* the two lost pirates ran into its hairy legs and hit the ground with a *THUMP*.

"What's it doing? whispered Boz-Eye as it lifted one leg slightly.

PPPAAAARRRPPPPP!!!

the monster sighed with a grin as the sound rippled down the corridor.

"BLITHERING BARNACLES" squealed Boz-Eye Bert as the green fog wafted up to his nostrils and out through his ears. His eyes whizzed around and around like a spinning top so fast they almost flew out.

"Oh blimey, was that you?" spluttered Three-Toes Magee, "I told you not to eat that cooked rat last night, I said it looked a funny colour."

"I can't breathe, everything's fuzzy, and I think my nose hairs have shrivelled up and dropped out" shrieked Boz-Eyed Bert.

"Quick check the belt thingy there might be something in there" squeaked Three-Toes as he pinched his nose closed.

Rummaging around in a stinky panic Boz-Eye started pulling out item after item from the stolen belt. A half-eaten chocolate bar, a black pen thing

113

that had a red clicky light on the end when you pressed a button and a black disk.

"Useless" shrieked Boz-Eye throwing them to the floor as he began to feel faint.

"Try another pocket" cried Three-Toes. Fumbling around Boz-Eye pulled out a ball. Three-Toes pointed at it excitedly "Put that in its bottom that will stop it" he cried jumping up and down.

"No way, you put it in" cried Boz-Eye as they threw it back and forth when suddenly it dropped to the floor.

Poof an explosion of pink dust went off startling the monster *PPPAAAARRRPPPPP!* and causing them to cough and splutter even more. "*AAAAARRRGGGHHHH,* girlie dust" cried Boz-Eye "we're going to be turned into fluffy fairy girls."

114

'Hold on I found something," cried Three-Toes as he pulled from the pocket a pair of black gloves and waved them in the pink and green cloudy air.

"Hurry hold them across your nose before we suffocate from the pong" cried Boz-Eye. Both pirates quickly slapped the gloves to their faces and breathed a sigh of relief.

"Look at that I don't even have to hold it, it's stuck right there on my face," said Three-Toes in amazement holding his hands away as the glove stayed put. "Look yours does the same, how clever is that, instant pong protection."

From the passage in front came a loud howl. The monster turned towards the sound and started to plod away in search of its nightmare friend.

"Did you hear that?" whispered Boz-Eye from beneath his sticky glove. Three-Toes nodded making his magic stuck on glove waggle on his face like a tiny octopus. "That's the captain you can bet my left eyeball on it. Come on hurry up, like it or not we need to stay behind our stinky friend."

****

Slowly the door opened, and out crept Fitz followed by Noggin and Snitch.

"Look, pink dust and some of my gadgets from my stolen belt" whispered Noggin quickly collecting them and putting them safely in her pockets.

"That means the pirates were here with the monster, and they went that way towards the vaults judging by the green trail," said Fitz

"But that's the same way we're going. Maybe we go a different way?" said Snitch hopefully as Fitz and Noggin took off after the monster. "I guess not" he moaned.

****

As Moonstone soared across Cloud Bay the streets below were empty.

"Words spread" cried Nift as the last few doors slammed shut and lights went out casting the town into darkness.

"At least everyone's safe for now," said Linc thankfully as they came to rest on the sand. "The monkeys seem to like the trees in Dolomite Dell so hopefully they won't spread this far."

"I don't think it's the monkeys we need to worry about" replied Sneak who was facing out across the cloud water.

"Have you ever seen the sea that colour?" asked Nift "and what is that?" as a large grey fin rose from the black thundery clouds, cutting through them for a moment then disappearing beneath.

117

****

Below the threatening cloud sea, the four dragons hovered in the air watching the large grey fin appear, circle then vanish. That was the only way they could get to the island from the caves, how could they do that with a giant shark prowling? With a deep rumble and a loud *CRRRAAAACK,* a bolt of lightning shot from the clouds above followed by another and another as a storm began to brew in the perilous waters around the shark.

There was no time to lose, they had to get through and to the island above. Ammolite flew forward and turned to face the others, her rainbow mirrored scales shone with every flash of light. She was the oldest and wisest of the Night Warriors dragons and the others followed her lead without question. With a nod, Heliodor and Nebular moved to either side of Ember to shield her.

Ammolite flew towards the thunderstorm, dodging the lightning bolts raining down and vanished. The three dragons watched from below as the storm raged on. With a crack of lightning, there was a colossal rumble and a red glow deep within the black clouds that got brighter before fading away. Another rumble and another, each followed by a glow, each from a different place in the cloud sea. The shark was chasing Ammolite, she was distracting it for the others to break through to safety.

Seeing their chance, the three dragons raced into the clouds. Inside the air was heavy and it was hard to see. The thunder rippled through the air vibrating on the dragon's wings as cold water soaked their scales. Up and up they flew heading for Cloud Bay when something caught their eye and they

119

screeched to a halt. Ammolite shot through the squall above them and giving chase was the gigantic two headed shark.

Motionless so as not to be seen, the others waited until they passed before shooting up and busting from the cloud sea to the island above.

Nift, Sneak, and Linc watched in amazement as the three dragons appeared like missiles with the clouds trailing from their wings. They dropped from the night sky and landed on the beach next to Moonstone.

"Ember, Heliodor, Nebular, oh thank goodness you're alright" cried Nift rushing towards them but the dragons did not hear, they were watching the waters behind them looking for the last dragon.

The rumbling got louder as the ground below shook and the black cloudy waters started to turn a deep shade of red. With a burst of fire, Ammolite rocketed from the sea into the sky and just below was the giant shark, both its mouths snapping at her tail.

With a whip of its body the shark made one last attempt to grab her before dropping from the air, and with an explosion of black clouds, disappeared back into the depths.

Ammolite landed on the beach with her wet scales shimmering, she was exhausted.

"Ammolite are you alright, what happened down there?" cried Nift running towards the brave dragon.

"Where is everyone?" asked Linc. "Where are the Night Warriors and where are Fitz, Noggin, and Snitch?"

The dragon's heads lifted, and all looked towards Dreamcast Mountain and the pirate ship hovering above it.

"'They're inside," said Nift following the dragon's gaze. "They're inside the mountain with the others *WAHOO*!!!"

CHAPTER 10

Kaboom

Deep inside the mountain, the corridor outside the vault was becoming a little crowded. Bysidian and Quillion stood firm by the vault door blocking the way for Solomon Fear, the wolf, and the pirates. Behind them stood the three remaining Night Warriors swords drawn, facing the motley crew of raggedy Pirates.

"Well look what we have here, a pirate sandwich," said Templar Storm with a grin.

"Not for me thank you, I have the feeling it would be a bit chewy and bitter" replied Lucius.

"And it would get stuck in your teeth" finished Fabian Feldspar. "You would be sucking on bits of chewy pirates for weeks, *yuck*."

The voices of his team beyond the pirates came as a great relief to Bysidian. He would never show fear to anyone, especially his men but he had begun to wonder how just Quillion and himself would stand any chance against all those pirates and the wolf.

"I think you will find you're surrounded," he said to Solomon Fear not moving his eyes for a second from the pirate captain, as there was no trust between them.

"Oh, now that's where you are wrong" smirked the pirate his golden tooth twinkling. "What was it you Night Warriors say, 'You will never lose the battle if you stay one step ahead' and they are wise words."

Crashing through the darkness, the monster appeared stumbling towards them all.

"Finally, look Bert we found them" cried Three-Toes Magee as he and Boz-Eyed Bert barged past the monster hoping to join the other pirates. They stopped in their tracks when standing between them they saw the three Night Warriors.

"What is that smell?" cried Lucius screwing up his nose in disgust as the two pong covered Pirates pointed the blame at each other.

This was the distraction Solomon Fear had been waiting for. "NOW" he bellowed as the huge spider hiding on the ceiling spun down a line. It wrapped around Bysidian and Quillion, encasing them in a sticky cocoon, leaving them dangling in the air unable to move their arms or legs.

At the same moment, the monster lunged at the three Night Warriors who were standing in his way.

PPPPPPPPPAAAAAARRRPPPP!

"Oh no not again!" wailed Boz-Eyed Bert as in a haze of green foul smelling fog Lucius, Templar, and Fabian ran towards the monster.

"Sky-High get your sorry butt up here right now." Sky-High Charlie pushed his way through the pirates and under the wolf to join the captain.

"She's all yours" Solomon Fear grinned as he backed away a safe distance.

"Why thank you" grinned the scrawny pirate as he walked towards the vault door swinging his sticks of dynamite by the fuse around faster and faster.

Helplessly dangling off the ground Bysidian and Quillion watched as he wedged several sticks around the door.

"One-two-three-four...*KABOOM*" he sniggered as he pushed them in.

"You're going to regret this believe me" yelled Bysidian. "I know who you are and what you're thinking, remember" he yelled, but Solomon Fear just laughed.

"Oh, I'm so scared, big brave Night Warriors all stuck up in an incy wincy spiders web" he cackled as Sky-High lit the fuses one by one.

"FIRE IN THE HOLE" he yelled as he ran back between the wolf's legs and covered one ear with his remaining hand, (the missing arm, well that's a story for another day).

The explosion propelled the iron door clean off its hinges leaving it in a crumpled mass of twisted metal. The blast shot down the corridor covering the wolf and the pirates in dust and rubble, making them drop to the floor as it slammed Bysidian and Quillion hard into the stone walls.

127

Surprised, the monster stopped for a moment as the rush of wind and debris bounced off its face.

"BYSIDIAN, QUILLION WE'RE COMING" yelled Templar as he Lucius and Fabian battled with the enormous monster.

"WE'RE IN LADS" cried Solomon Fear as with a cheer the pirates rushed below the wolf and poured into the Granite Vault.

****

Hiding in the shadows waiting for the right moment were Fitz and his team. If they were seen by the pirates they risked being caught before they could get to the precious Dream Catcher Pearls.

"We have to do something" whispered Noggin as helplessly they watched the three Night Warriors battle with the monster. With swipes of its hairy arms, it was crashing them into the corridor walls one after another.

"I know, and we will, but if we get caught, we are no use to Bysidian and his men. Be patient we just need the right moment to make a break for the vault," said Fitz.

That moment came sooner than expected when an almighty $BOOM$ rattled down the corridor as the pirates blew the doors off. The monster turned its attention towards the noise and away from the Night Warriors, they saw their chance. Templar, Lucius, and Fabian attacked together catching the monster off guard.

"Look they're winning, they're winning," said Snitch as the monster began to fade.

"That's it, the monsters weak now's our chance," said Fitz as he ran towards the fight.

"Come on let's go," said Noggin running after him.

129

"Oh no, let's not" wailed Snitch as he stayed put for a moment before realising, he was now all alone and chased after them.

As they reached the monster it disappeared in a swirl of dust, the Night Warriors had won. "Keep going" yelled Fitz as the others followed him through the dusty air with its distinctive pong.

"What are you doing here?" yelled Templar Storm, "I told you to get somewhere safe."

"And as we said, we can help, *come on*" yelled Fitz as the Night Warriors joined them running towards the blast.

With monster dust floating in the air, they all screeched to a halt. The giant wolf was stood before them blocking the corridor.

The three Night Warriors lifted their swords ready to attack when a voice stopped them.

"STOP….this one's mine," hollered Noggin walking forward.

130

"Hello puppy dog" she smiled "do you remember us?"

"Honestly I think she has lost her marbles," said Snitch "Puppy, that's not a puppy it's a great big killer white wolf."

"What *is* she doing?" asked Fabian. "We can't let her tackle this thing alone, it will eat her in one gulp. This is our job."

"Oh, just you wait and see, do not underestimate the power of Noggin," replied Fitz with a grin.

"So, puppy do you want to play?" asked Noggin twirling her grappling hook in her hand. With this, the wolf swished its tail and pounced. In an instant Noggins grappling hook was flying through the air, around and around it went winding the wolf in its line before it crashed to the ground with a *thump* unable to move.

"I thank you," said Noggin with a bow towards the three open mouthed Night Warriors. There was

131

a *poof* of pink dust as she followed this with launching a dust bomb to celebrate.

"Oh, now you are just being dramatic, show off" huffed Snitch trying to sound unimpressed.

"Wow," said Lucius Squall " have you ever thought of training as a Night Warrior?"

"Well, it is funny you should mention that…." started Noggin as the three warriors ran past her.

"There they are, come on," said Templar as they ran towards their web bound leader and teammate.

"STOP, STOP" yelled Bysidian. "Above us, right above us, there is a giant spider stay back."

Watching every movement, the spider was ready to pounce on them. The sound of pirates inside the vault rung out into the corridor as they ran around the Granite Vault aiming for the Nightmare Vault beyond.

"We need to hurry," said Bysidian they are almost there and if they get inside and free more nightmares..." he shook his head in anger.

"Flashcrash?" whispered Noggin to Fitz and Snitch.

"What?" said Templar. "What are you whispering about, do you have an idea?" as the spider turned to look at him.

"Sort of" replied Noggin in a whisper. "If it can't see us then we have a chance."

"Please don't tell me you have something to make us invisible in that magic belt" whispered Lucius "because if you do, I have to get me one of those."

"Not quite, but you may want to close your eyes," said Noggin moving her hand very slowly towards her belt pockets. In her grasp, she felt the round shape of a Flashcrash grenade. Slipping her finger inside the pin she took a deep breath. "All of you close your eyes now."

Yanking the grenade from her pocket she pulled the pin and threw it as high as she could. There was a blinding light causing the wolf to yelp and the spider to squeal as it shrivelled away in pain.

The light vanished leaving the spider and wolf blinded. "It won't last long so we have to hurry," said Fitz. One swipe of the warrior's swords was all it took to cut the web binding and free the spiders' prisoners.

"Hey, Three-Toes catch" came the cry from inside the vault as a Dream Catcher Pearl rolled out the vault door and stopped when it bumped into Fitz's boot.

This was followed by the sound of running feet, "For seaweed's sake, how many times do I have to tell you Boz-Eye catch is no fun. You have to throw the ball *to* me, not to the other two of me you can see with your wonky eyes," said Three-Toes Magee as he ran out of the vault chasing the stray pearl. Grinding to a halt he froze "Uh, oh" he declared before taking a few steps backwards and running back inside.

"Hey, that's one of my Sticky Gloves," called Noggin after him.

"Well, this will do nicely," said Fitz picking up the pearl. "You all carry on, I will be right behind you."

As they charged into the vault a familiar rush of cold air followed by a sucking noise and a loud howl came from outside before Fitz strolled in behind them.

"There one wolf and one spider back where they belong," he said throwing the now black pearl into the air and catching it like a ball whilst returning Noggins grappling hook.

135

The sight before him brought Fitz to a standstill. The Granite Vault was filled with pirates hanging from the rows of pearls spiralling around the room. They were pulling pearls from their place and throwing them down to others below who were playing football, juggling with them or simply throwing them to the ground smashing them for fun.

Bysidian and his team were in the midst of it with pirates running at them from every direction, whilst pearls rained down being thrown as weapons

"Fitz over here" yelled Noggin who was climbing up the nearest row of pearls whilst dodging pirates. Snitch was stood below cowering from the fight, surrounded by shattered pearl pieces. "How many do we need?" she called.

Fitz thought back quickly to Maisie's nightmare. "The monster, wolf, and spider are gone" he called "that leaves the two headed shark and the monkeys. "Two Noggin, we need two."

"Two it is" she called back as she grabbed the nearest pearl and pulled it free from the others.

"Here Snitch, hold this'" Fitz said handing the wolf and spider filled pearl to Snitch.

"What am I supposed to do with this" he squealed holding it out as if it were about to explode."

"Put it in your pocket keep it safe," replied Fitz.

"Catch" yelled Noggin as she dropped the first pearl to Fitz who jammed it into his pocket and looked up ready for the next. With two Dream Catcher Pearls safely stored he called to Noggin "come on we need to get out of here."

"Men, we need to find Solomon Fear, can anyone see him?" Bysidian ordered as he deflected a flying pearl aiming for his head whilst fighting off the pirate chewing at his armoured leg.

137

Across the vault Fitz saw the scared pirate from the corridor outside, running into the shadows and towards the Nightmare Vault.

"He's at the Nightmare Vault" Fitz cried.

"We need to stop him *now*" yelled Bysidian as he broke free from the pirate attackers and ran towards the shadows.

The blast blew him backwards slamming him into the wall beside Fitz and his team as his cloak pooled around him. The other Night Warriors were blown clean off their feet along with the hoard of pirates as the rush of wind and wreckage flew towards them.

"He's in, he's inside the Nightmare Vault come on" cried Bysidian rushing to his feet and running from sight. In a flash his battered and bruised men followed and close behind were the gang of pirates.

Noggin jumped up and was about to follow them all when Fitz grabbed her arm.

"No stop," he said chocking from the dust "we need to help the island outside and leave Bysidian and his men to do their job. We need to protect the other Dream Drifters."

"You go, you and Snitch it doesn't need all three of us, you have the pearls you need, and the Night Warriors could use my help," she said patting her belt and pulling free of Fitz's grasp.

"No Noggin we're a team, we don't split up" cried Snitch.

"I have to Snitch, I have to help. We can help more if we split up trust me."

"She's right," said Fitz listening to the sound of clashing swords and pirates cheering beyond. "Snitch we have to go and get these pearls out of here. If we capture the other nightmare's then we can *all* stop the pirates."

139

Snitch looked at Noggin with teary eyes "just be careful ok?"

"Promise," replied Noggin ruffling his hair and then she ran from sight towards the battle beyond.

"Alright Snitch time to be brave. The sooner we capture the other nightmares the sooner we are back to help. Let's go," said Fitz.

CHAPTER 11

PSSSSSTTTTT!

Dashing from the Granite Vault into the passageways outside Fitz and Snitch ran as fast as they could. Doors opened as they approached with Guardian's faces appearing to see who was coming. "Back inside, stay inside" called Fitz "it's not safe yet."

As one door opened Snitch stopped "here take this *please*" he whispered handing over the black pearl from his pocket containing the wolf and spider. "Put it somewhere safe, there are some *bad* things inside." The Guardian nodded and carried the pearl cautiously back inside.

"Phew" sighed Snitch as he caught up with Fitz, "am I glad that's gone if it had cracked open in my trouser pocket that spider could have crawled anywhere ..." he shivered at the thought.

Fitz and Snitch stopped at the bottom of a tunnel slide. "This is the way they got in so it's our way out, ready?"

"As ready as I'll ever be" replied Snitch as they started to climb. Three steps forward and one step back they climbed the slippery slide, around and around until they could see a small circle of light above.

"There look, the top," said Snitch. With relief, they clambered out and stood to catch their breath. The dragons landing area was empty and way above them they could just make out 'The Swirling Pearl' bobbing in the night sky.

"There, the pirate's ropes we can climb out on those," said Snitch running for the closest one.

142

"Snitch, no stop we can't use them if we start to climb their ropes the pirates on the ship will see them moving and spot us. We need another way and quickly."

As they stood thinking a tiny light appeared then another and another. Bright dancing white lights that twinkled and crackled like moving ice. They got closer and closer lighting up Fitz and Snitch's faces with their cold blue glow.

"Frost Fairies," said Snitch as one got closer. A tiny delicate fairy shimmering in blue and white with wings as thin as spider webs sparkling in a morning frost.   The surrounding mountainsides began to glisten and sparkle as trails of ice from blue Ice Imps appeared.

"They must have returned home and seen the ship," said Fitz "but I am not sure what they can do to help."

143

As they drew closer Snitch took in a sharp breath "Look, look what they're doing" as they weaved through the air and across the mountain rocks.

Slowly but surely a ladder built from ice started to appear, longer and longer the icicles and frost crystals bound together building it rung by rung until it reached the two tiny Dream Drifters below.

"Maybe they *can* help," said Snitch. "Do you think Embers out there waiting for us?" he asked as they began to climb.

"I hope so," said Fitz.

Just below the floating ship they stopped, the Ice Imps and Frost Fairies by their sides.

"How many are on the boat still?" whispered Fitz to Snitch who clapped his hands together quietly and looked above through his Seeker Glasses.

"At least ten, and they are all over the place. How on earth are we going to get out of the mountain top without being seen? We could sure do with one of Noggins gadgets as a distraction right about now" he sighed worrying about their teammate left below.

PSSSSSTTTTTTTTT...

Fitz looked up then down.

"Did you hear that?" he whispered

"Yes, I did, and you could have held it in, you are almost as bad as that stinky monster" snapped Snitch.

"I thought it was you" replied Fitz

PPPPPSSSSSSSSTTTTT...

"Where is that coming from?" said Fitz puzzled as his fingers started freezing to the ladder.

"There look up" pointed Snitch as a blue fluffy face with a big red nose appeared over the mountain top.

"*PSSSSTTTTT*" it called and waved being careful not to be seen. It was joined by another face and another when suddenly a small piece of ice fell and landed on Fitz's face. As it started to melt, he scooped it into his hand.

"Hailstones, Snitch I think we may just have the distraction we need."

Slowly Fitz and Snitch started to climb and as they reached the top the Hail Hurlers aimed at the ship and the crew aboard. A torrent of ice and hail hurtled towards the ship, faster and faster bouncing off the sails and cannons.

"OUCH, OUCH, RUN, RUN" cried the pirates. "We're under attack, ice attack, RUN FOR YOUR LIVES" they cried as they slipped around, taking cover from the stinging hail that was gathering like small snowdrifts on deck.

With the pirate's busy Fitz and Snitch leapt from the ladder and out of the top of Dreamcast Mountain. They scrambled down the icy mountain face and came to rest only when they were in the safety of the snow covered villages below. Following were the Frost Fairies and Ice Imps, and behind them, giggling mischievously were the Hail Hurlers.

"Oh, thank you, thank you, thank you" puffed Snitch as he hopped from foot to foot and hugged himself tightly trying to keep warm.

"That was amazing, what he said and thank you again," said Fitz looking at the creatures gathered around him. The air was so bitterly cold he started to shiver, and his breath felt like it was freezing as it left his nose and mouth.

"I-I-I c-c-can't f-f-f-eel m-m-my f-f-feet" stuttered Snitch turning a shade of blue with ice crystals hanging in his spikey hair. Fitz couldn't feel his feet either and the numb feeling was rising in his legs.

"Please see me, please, please, see me" he whispered with shaking hands pulling the Dream Catcher Pearl from his pocket. Holding it high it shone like a beacon in the ferocious blizzard whirling around them.

****

"Ember where are you going?" called Nift startled as the red dragon suddenly flew from the beach without warning.

She had seen it, a faint light high up on the mountain and he knew exactly who it was. Her eyes never left the glow getting closer and closer as she fought through the snow that melted as it hit her warm scales.

Just as the light faded, Ember rose from the blizzard to see Fitz and Snitch huddled together in deep snow. Startled the Frost Fairies, Ice Imps and Hail Hurlers ran for cover in their houses, scared by the fiery red demon that had arrived in their village.

"Here lads, what's that going on down there?" came the shout aboard ship. The pirates had returned above deck after the Hail Hurlers attack and had seen the glow from the pearl.

"A dragon, a dragon it's them, it's some of those horrible little Dream Drifters. They must have come out the mountain, stop them" as they started throwing everything they could. Plates, cups, bits of old rope, one of those umbrellas you get in fancy drinks, an old boot and even a wooden leg came tumbling down crashing into the snow.

Hastily Ember landed and with all their remaining strength the almost frozen Fitz and Snitch clambered aboard. They collapsed in the saddle unable to hold on properly as Ember took off and dived from the mountain to the island below.

The further they dropped, the warmer the air became, and as the ice and snow on them melted they started to regain the feeling in their feet and hands. Ember's scales glowed fiery red, warming her passengers as until they were thawed and warm through. Passing over Dolomite Dell they could see the monkeys still causing mayhem and mischief.

"At least we know where the monkeys went now" called Fitz.

As they approached the beach, they saw Linc, Nift, and Sneaker jumping around, and waving madly surrounded by the Night Warriors dragons. A large *splash* in the cloud sea followed by a huge

150

fin made Snitch gulp, "and I think we found the two headed shark."

"HEY" called Fitz as they circled above, thankful they were safe.

"HEY YOURSELF" called back Nift. "Boy, are we glad to see you."

"We need to get back to Dolomite Dell and help everyone, but we have a present for you" called Fitz as he dropped a Dream Catcher Pearl into her hands.

"The sharks all yours. No, honestly there is no need to thank us" shouted Snitch with a grin as they flew away.

Linc looked at his team, "so who wants to be the bait?"

****

Ember landed on the outskirts of Dolomite Dell as quietly as she could.

"Wait here girl we'll be back as soon as we can'" said Fitz slipping from her saddle. Clambering through the trees and undergrowth trying not to be seen by the monkeys, Fitz and Snitch snuck behind a large tree trunk and watched the commotion before them.

There were monkeys everywhere running along the streets banging on doors and windows and hanging on the rooftops. The trees shook as they jumped from branch to branch and they splashed in the stream whilst chasing the tiny Dew Dancers, who were desperately trying to hide.

"Ok Snitch we've got one pearl left. We need to find the central point of the monkeys, if we can get to the middle, I think I can capture them all at once" he whispered.

With a clap of his gloves, Snitch's Seeker Glasses came to life. Looking around every monkey appeared as his glasses glowed with their heat.

"Wow they are *everywhere*" he gasped in a quiet voice as one swung above them in the tree canopy making leaves rain down. "There, the stone bridge over the stream they are all around it.".

"The stone bridge it is then" replied Fitz. "We just need to try and get there unnoticed if at all possible so stay behind me Snitch and whatever you do don't make a sound."

BAM! a bouncing beetle flew through the air and hit the tree they were hiding behind causing it to rebound hard and hit Snitch in the head. "*OWWWWW!!!*" he cried at the top of his lungs "*THAT HURT.*"

Fitz turned to him with horror on his face "Snitch *SSSHHHH*" he hissed.

"IT'S IN MY HAIR, GET IT OUT, GET IT OUT" he squealed running around shaking his head as the black beetle got tangled in his spikey hair.

BAM! another beetle bounced towards him and bopped him right on the nose then uncurled and hung on his glasses staring at him curiously through the lenses. *"AARRGGHHHHHH, I'M UNDER ATTACK HELP ME"* he screeched as he tripped over a branch and landed face first on the woodland floor.

Squelch, he put his gloved hand down on something gooey and slippery and cold. *"I HAVE POO ON ME"* he cried *"MONKEY POO ON ME… AARRGGHHHHHH I'M GOING TO BE SICK"* he shouted as a Squidgeable slug squeezed from under his hand and started to glide away, still in the shape of Snitch's handprint.

"Snitch, Snitch stop it, stop it the monkeys will hear you" shushed Fitz as he yanked the beetle from Snitch's hair and flicked the one away from his glasses.

"*Ouch*, hey that hurt as well" moaned Snitch rolling onto his back shaking in alarm and trying to get his breath.

"Listen," said Fitz "the noise has stopped," but Snitch wasn't listening he was staring at the treetops and all the brown hairy faces staring down on them.

"Whoops," he whimpered as the rabble of monkeys started climbing towards them.

"CHANGE OF PLAN, HOLD ONTO SOMETHING TIGHT," shouted Fitz as he held out the Dream Catcher Pearl and ripped it open.

As the wind howled around them faster and faster Snitch suddenly felt something hard and round shoot up one of his trouser legs, followed by

155

another and another. With his eyes tight shut, he screamed as something wet and slimy shot up the other leg and crawled into his sock, followed by more gathering around his knees.

The screeching monkeys were all trying to run but it was too late, they were sucked one by one into the Dream Catcher Pearl and as the last one's tail disappeared inside Fitz slammed the pearl shut.

Silence...

No, wait...

AAAAAAARRRRRRRRGGGGG HHHHHHHHHHHHHH!!!!!!!

Snitch was still screaming as he jumped to his feet. He had leaves and twigs in his hair making him look like a scarecrow as he proceeded to jump around like his pants were on fire.

"THEY ARE IN MY TROUSERS, GET THEM OUT BEFORE THEY REACH MY JINGLY JANGLY BITS" he screamed as he jumped up and down in front of Fitz who was laughing loudly.

"Come here stop running around and just keep still," he said placing the Nightmare Pearl full of monkeys beside him.

Snitch tried to stand still the best he could as several Squidgeable Slugs slipped from one leg and bouncing beetles from the other.

"Oh no you don't," said Fitz as they tried to glide and bounce away. Catching them he placed them in his pockets and fastened them in.

"What are you doing?" asked Snitch who had removed his sock and was pouring the last slippery stray slug out of it.

"These little guys may just come in handy you never know. I wonder why they didn't get sucked into the pearl like the others?"

"*BECAUSE THEY WERE STUCK IN MY PANTS*" wailed Snitch loudly with a shudder.

FITZ, SNITCH, WHERE ARE YOU?" came the shout from beyond the trees.

"OVER HERE," called back Fitz as he and Snitch clambered through the undergrowth and out into the streets of Dolomite Dell.

Linc, Nift, and Sneaker were waiting with the dragons Moonstone, Heliodor, Nebular, and Ammolite.

"Look, a matching pair," said Linc holding out the shark filled Nightmare Pearl and looking at the black pearl in Fitz's hands.

"Oh, I could make a lovely pair of earrings from these" chuckled Nift.

A rustling in the undergrowth made them turn as an unimpressed Ember appeared. She had a large streak of purple slime on her head as a slug slipped down her neck whilst hanging on her tail were two black shiny beetles.

"Oh, who are these little fellows?" asked Nift as she held out her hand for the rainbow coloured slug to slide into. The beetles bounced away as the slug curled up in her warm hand and went to sleep. "Oh, how cute, look," she gushed.

"*Cute, honestly*?" said Snitch flabbergasted. "You want to try having one in your sock or up your trouser legs then we will see how cute they are, and why are you dripping wet?"

"Well this little guy is coming home with me and I shall call him Humphry" as she slipped the slug into her pocket, "and why I'm wet, well it's a long story but it involves an extremely stubborn shark" she replied.

159

A large drip of purple glittery slime, courtesy of Humphry, slid down Ember's nose and dribbled into her nostril making her sneeze hard.

PLINK! PLINK! PLINK the glass frogs hiding in the warmth of her scales all shot out with a blast and bounced off the Dream Drifters before smashing on the floor. Each changed into a small duplicate frog and hopped away with a splash as they jumped into the babbling stream.

"Ah, that will be the frogs, I must have missed them as well," mumbled Fitz his cheeks going red with embarrassment.

"Err, hold on, where's Noggin?" interrupted Sneaker.

"Doing what she does best," said Fitz, "causing chaos."

Chapter 12

The Scent of Old Lavender

Leaping over the remains of the exploded door Noggin burst into the Nightmare Vault. The damp air filled her lungs instantly and the cold made her shudder. Before her, a colossal battle was revealed as the pirates fought to stop the Night Warriors reaching Solomon Fear and destroying his plan.

Swords clashed with sparks in the dark as the pirates, with scarves around their faces, defied the pearls powers reaching them. Others were not so lucky and were either screaming in terror, crying uncontrollably or shouting in ferocious anger at each other.

Beyond his rabble of pirates, Solomon Fear was just in sight, a circle of pirates around him like a shield. He was shouting orders to others who were scaling the black pearl strands that wound around the vault walls.

"THAT ONE, YES CAREFULLY NOW" he shouted as a pirate reached for a pearl before him and dropped it down to the others. "NOW THAT ONE, NO THE ONE ABOVE" he ordered to another. "THAT'S RIGHT, THAT'S RIGHT, CAREFUL WITH THEM BOYS."

Across the room, Bysidian saw Noggin appear and with a punch to the pirate hanging on his back he ran toward her.

"What are you doing here Noggin, I told you to get out of the mountain," he said as a screaming pirate launched themselves at his leg and tried to bite him through his boots.

"I can help Bysidian, I can help. I have gadgets and things they won't expect."

"Is there just you?" he asked kicking the pirate from his leg who ran away giggling like a naughty child.

"Yes, the others have gone to help everyone on the island. They have Dream Catcher Pearls and can trap the nightmares" she replied as fat tears started to roll down her cheeks.

Grabbing the bottom of his cloak Bysidian tore off a strip and tied it around Noggin's mouth and nose to stop her breathing in the evil air.

"Honestly Noggin you are so brave but stupid it scares me and amazes me at the same time," he said. "Keep that mask on and under no circumstances take it off" he ordered. With this and a cry of "GERONIMO" two pirates appeared from mid-air and landed on Bysidian's back dragging him back to battle.

"Well, well, well, what do we have here?' said a croaky voice as a filthy pirate with scabs on his face and ring in his nose appeared. "You're one of those measly Dream Drifters we caught earlier" he cackled through his cloth covered mouth. "Haven't you had enough? What do you think someone as pathetic as you will do to this powerful crew?" he said waving his hand towards the pirates.

Startled Noggin stumbled back and tripped which made the pirate cackle even louder. "You can't even stand on your own two feet never mind fight" he screeched and grabbed for Noggins leg. With an almighty yank, Noggin pulled her leg free and left him holding her boot.

"PATHETIC, PATHETIC" she shouted as she grabbed a dust bomb from her belt. "I'll show you pathetic" as she threw it towards the pirate, and it jammed on his large gold nose ring. With a *poof,*

it exploded filling the air and the pirates face with thick pink dust.

"AARRGGHHHHHH" he cried as Noggin ran towards him and yanked off the cloth covering his mouth. "Let's see who's pathetic now" she snapped as he took in a deep gasp and started to wail like a tiny baby.

"Yep I thought so" grinned Noggin putting her boot back on as the pirate ran from the vault blubbering.

Under the cover of the pink dust, Noggin ran around grabbing the pirates face masks from them. When the dust finally cleared each ran from the vault as the nightmares seized hold of their emotions.

"CHAAAARGE," a small group of pirates ran towards her. She pulled a Flashcrash grenade from her belt and pulled the pin.

"That's it, look right here" she called as she threw the grenade into the air and covered her eyes. *Boom!* the grenade exploded, with a brilliant burst of light.

Dazed and confused the blinded pirates ran around in circles before smashing into each other and knocking themselves out.

"Well that worked better than expected," she said jumping over them on the floor and running towards the battle when she stopped, something caught her eye in the shadows.

"*Shush*, this way over here Bert. If we are quick, we can get out and no one will even notice" came the voice Noggin recognised from somewhere.

"I am following you stupid, I just don't know which one of you I should be following" replied Boz-Eyed Bert with his eyes facing in two directions as usual.

166

"Here look give it to me before you drop it and we are all in trouble," said Three-Toes Magee as he snatched a Nightmare Pearl from Bert's hands. "Tell me again why we need this one anyway, the boss didn't ask for it?"

"Because if we take an extra one for him then we will be in his good books, see? We're being smart Three-Toes and using our brains, besides I like this one it's like it was calling to me."

"Well let's just get out of here, I do not fancy getting involved in that," said Three-Toes pointing towards the battle as an old boot flew across the room and hit the wall above his head. Grabbing Boz-Eyed Bert by the arm they ran for the vault door.

"Oh no you don't," said Noggin as her grappling gun shot across the fleeing pirate's path and jammed in the rock walls.

Focused on their escape and not on the line that was at ankle height below them, the two pirates tripped and flew through the air. Like slow motion they wriggled and grasped at the black pearl that launched from Three-Toes grasp before it hit the floor with a *CRACK*, followed by a *THUMP* from the flying pirates.

"Oh, now you've gone and done it," they cried getting to their feet as the thick black fog started to drift from the broken pearl. "Well I'm not hanging around to find out what comes out," said Boz-Eyed Bert.

"Me neither" cried Three-Toes Magee as they ran for it leaving Noggin staring at the pearl in horror.

"NOGGIN, WHAT HAVE YOU DONE?" came the shout from Bysidian.

"It wasn't me honest," she said as the crack grew, and a dazzling light shone out followed by a

large shadow heaving its way through the split.
The black fog got thicker and thicker making many
of the pirates turn and run in fear.

"HURRY, HURRY UP AND GRAB THE
LAST ONE, THEY'RE COMING" shouted
Solomon Fear as the Night Warriors charged
through the remaining few.

Dropping the last stolen pearl in his shoulder
bag Solomon Fear turned to face them.

"Drop the bag" ordered Bysidian Black "there's
no escape now you're trapped."

"Oh, now see that's where you're wrong," said
the captain with a grin as his gaze lifted upwards
and he pointed behind them.

As the scent of old lavender wafted through the
vault the Night Warriors slowly turned to face the
massive shadow behind them. She was so tall she
had to bend her head to stand up but with the

169

slopping of her lips and the sucking of her false teeth, they knew exactly who it was.

"No, please not again, I still have nightmares from last time" wailed Lucius as the giant Kissing Granny appeared blocking the vault door as she shuffled towards them.

Granny's grey hair was pulled into a tight bun and on the tip of her nose were perched a pair of purple rimmed glasses she peered down through. A pair of pearl earrings hung from her saggy ear lobes with a matching string around the neck of her flowery dress and knitted cardigan. Her wrinkled stockings gathered around her ankles stopping where they met her comfortable red velvet slippers.

"Now my lovelies why are you all fighting and shouting, that's not nice, someone will get hurt," she said waving her finger at them with its red painted nail. "Is anyone hurt, do you need me to kiss you better?" she asked puckering up her red painted lips and showing the bits of lipstick caught on her false teeth.

"No, we're fine, all fine thank you" called back Templar Storm.

"Look at you all dressed up in your knight's armour with toy swords don't you look cute? Oh, dear but look at you," she said peering at a pirate through her glasses. "You're all dirty you need your face washing young man, now stay still," she said as she licked her finger and with the slippery dribble wiped the terrified pirates face.

"Bless me you're all dirty little scallywags," she said looking around. "What have you been up to? Well I'm just going to have to clean you all up but first I think each of you needs a lovely kiss," she said and licked her lips, so they glistened with drool.

171

AARRGGHHHHHH.... the pirates took off in every direction banging into each other to escape the lips smacking towards them.

"Let me out, get out of here, RUN FOR YOUR LIVES."

In all the pandemonium, Solomon Fear used the diversion to disappear.

"Where is he, where is he, do you see him?" shouted Bysidian pushing away pirates stumbling into him.

"THERE" cried Fabian pointing towards the Kissing Granny's wrinkled stockings. Clambering unnoticed up her wrinkles was Solomon Fear, the bag of stolen Nightmare Pearls swinging from his back. With his long black coat swaying and his sword tucked into his belt he clambered up her dress and to her knitted cardigan, before reaching her pocket and dropping inside.

The vault rung with the sound of squealing pirates being picked up and kissed leaving them with huge red lipstick prints on their faces and dribble running down their chins. Some had fainted from the shock and were being dragged out by others who had escaped.

"Come on, we have to stop him follow me," ordered Bysidian as they ran for the stockings and started to climb.

"*OUCH! OUCH!* hey, what do you think you're doing?" came the cry as the granny stopped chasing the pirates and looked down with a frown. As the Night Warriors hung on, she reached down and picked them off her legs one by one, standing them in a row on the floor.

"Now what do you have to say for yourselves?" she asked with a stern finger. They looked at each other confused and shrugged. "You hurt me with your sharp toy swords and that pointy armour, look

173

what you did." With that, she pulled one of her stockings down to reveal a leg that was so hairy it looked like a gorilla's.

"There look, see you have hurt me" showing them some tiny scratches. "Now you should know better young man," she said pointing at Bysidian who stood still not knowing what to say. "I think you boys need to think about your actions and need some time out" as she turned them to face the wall. "You stay there and think about what it is you have done."

There came a chuckling from her pocket as Solomon Fear listened in. Whilst the granny was distracted the pirates had all slowly slipped out of the vault's door scurrying away down the corridors.

"Where has everyone gone?" she asked pushing her false teeth back in with her tongue. "Aha I know, oh this is my favourite game, hide and seek. What fun, ready or not here I come," she said as spit flew from her lips and she shuffled out of the vault door. As she left the room Solomon Fear peeped out of her pocket and with a partly chewed toffee stuck to his hat waved to the Night Warriors.

"She told us off," said Lucius. "She can't do that can she?"

"Oh stop being such a baby" snapped Bysidian. "Come on we have to stop Solomon escaping."

Charging out into the corridor they ran after the granny disappearing into the distance.

"Who's that?" asked Templar looking at the small figure hanging from her tights.

"Oh   no,   Noggin"   sighed   Bysidian.

Chapter 13

A Half Sucked Boiled Sweet

Along the corridors, the granny went opening doors looking for her playmates. Screams echoed as she found unsuspecting Guardians and planted big kisses on them leaving lipstick in their white hair and beards.

"Here I come" she called out "I'm getting warmer I can feel it, lookout, lookout wherever you are." Noggin clambered a little higher up her leg and held on tight.

"Well now a game of tag, we are full of beans today" as the Night Warriors raced down the corridor towards her. "Come on then catch me if you can," she said shuffling away. Passing a tunnel slide the granny stopped, she could hear voices.

"Hurry up I can smell her all flowery and old, she's coming," as the sound of scrabbling and slipping feet rang out from up the tunnel. "*Shuusshhhh*" came the hiss as the noises suddenly stopped. *Squeakkkk* a pirate's foot slipped against the slide.

"Aha, found you" she called as she squeezed herself up the slide after them. With the shrieking and yelling of escaping pirates flowing from the tunnel, the Night Warriors gave chase.

As the pirates poured from the top of the slide, they ran for the ropes hanging from the ship waiting above.

"Wey hey lads, did we get them?" called the pirates onboard as they hung over the sides watching the others climb.

177

"MOVE, MOVE, GET OUT OF THE WAY, HIDE SHE'S COMING" they hollered loudly as they climbed as fast as they could.

"WHAT, WHO'S COMING AND WHERE'S THE CAPTAIN?"

That question was swiftly answered as the granny wriggled and squeezed her way out of the slide. With a *POP* she stood looking up at the dangling ropes full of fleeing pirates.

"Oh, now boys play fair, I'm too old for climbing ropes," she said stopping to catch her breath as she whistled through her loose teeth. "Come back and we can share a nice prune juice."

"You must be kidding lady" a pirate called down, "prune juice *ugh!*"

As the granny was busy with the pirate crew Solomon Fear climbed carefully from her pocket, reaching for a rope close by. Slowly he pulled it towards him and with a tight grip swung free whilst shaking bits of old screwed up tissue from his boots. Holding his breath, he waited to make sure she had not noticed before starting to climb. Watching him below was Noggin who was clambering up the flowery dress as fast as she could.

Bysidian and his team of Night Warriors ran out of the slide and screeched to a halt. The granny towered above them and above her pouring back onto 'The Swirling Pearl' were the pirates.

"Fear, where's Fear?" said Bysidian "he's the one we have to stop." At that moment a large half sucked boiled sweet fell to the floor beside them and smashed. Noggin was in the granny's pocket pointing frantically towards the captain now halfway up the rope.

"NO NOGGIN" cried Bysidian as she threw herself onto the rope and started to chase after him.

"We need help and quick, I hope those guys made it from the caves," said Templar Storm as he put two fingers in his mouth and whistled so loudly everyone stopped and looked at him, even the granny.

"Ah, you caught me you win" she smiled as she bent down towards him 'you all deserve a big kiss, come here with those squishy squashy cheeks."

"Any time now would be good," said Fabian watching the lips getting closer and closer.

The night sky suddenly filled with dragons. Ammolite, Heliodor, and Nebular had been joined by Quillion's dragon Crystalion, and with a streak of silver Bysidian's dragon Argent flew into view.

"Ugh no flies and insects, I CAN'T STAND FLIES" cried the granny batting them away. Reaching up she pulled herself out of the mountain top and vanished leaving the scent of lavender wafting in the air.

****

The last of the pirate crew heaved themselves onto 'The Swirling Pearls' deck and collapsed exhausted.

"No resting lads, come on the captains almost here *heave,*" as they grabbed the rope the captain and Noggin were climbing and began to pull.

"Out of my way, out of my way" bellowed Solomon Fear climbing aboard and pushing the pirates clear as he grabbed his sword.

Noggin stopped climbing and looked up at the ship full of pirates staring down at her.

"I wonder if Dream Drifters can fly?" he said with a glint of his golden tooth and with one swing of his blade chopped the rope.

Noggins screams of fear and anger filled the mountain as she fell.

181

"Hm, I guess not," he said with a shrug as his crew cheered.

"Right lads, time to go, let's get out of here I got what I wanted" as he took the bag full of Nightmare Pearls from his back. "Here grab hold of this and guard it with your lives," he said to the nearest pirates. "Ugh, what in the Krakens name happened to your eyes and what is that thing stuck on your nose?" he said screwing up his face in disgust at Boz-Eyed Bert.

"Nothing captain they've always been like this" replied Bert wincing in pain as he pulled the Sticky Glove from his face.

"Ouch, it's what makes him so special," added Three-Toes Magee peeling off his pong protector.

Before they could finish, Solomon Fear turned and ran across the deck to the wheel. Grabbing the serpent carved wood between his hands he cried "TO YOUR STATIONS LADS."

"AYE, AYE CAPTAIN" came the chorus as the crew took their positions and readied the ship to set sail.

"And where exactly do you think you are going?" came the voice from below as the Night Warriors appeared at the ship's side astride their faithful dragons and with them, Noggin.

Solomon Fear smirked and shook his head " Do you *ever* give up?" he said.

"*NEVER*" replied Bysidian as his men flew close around him. "But I think you should Solomon, admit it you seem to have lost this time. Now hand over the pearls before we make you and somebody gets hurt."

"Hurt, hurt" cackled the pirate "come on Bysidian we both know you would never truly hurt me, would you dear brother?"

"*Brother*" whispered Noggin in shock hanging onto Bysidian's cloak to steady herself in Argent's saddle.

"You are no brother of mine, you gave that right up when you turned to this life," snapped back Bysidian. "You have brought nothing but shame to me and the Night Warriors you deserted."

"Shame, don't talk to me about shame, call yourself a leader look at you all protective of those little Dream Drifters. You are supposed to battle nightmares and be a warrior not protect those wimps."

With that, a black shiny ball hit the flustered captain's hat knocking it to the floor before the bouncing beetle scurried off across the deck.

"Nice shot Snitch," said Fitz as Ember and Moonstone soared into view.

CHAPTER 14

Tug of War

The grey battered sails full of icy air whipping back and forth ready for the chase. Without taking his eyes off Bysidian, Solomon Fear tightened his grip on the wheel. The ship was straining to break free from the anchor holding it fast when with a clanking of the rusty chain it was released.

As fast as lightning the pirate captain heaved the wheel sharply to the left and the ship rolled sideways as it took off at tremendous speed.

"HANG ON TIGHT LADS THIS COULD GET CHOPPY" as they flew down the mountain aiming for escape at Cloud Bay.

The crew were thrown across the deck this way then that battling against the rolling ship as they manned their stations. The sky around the fleeing ship swarmed with dragons giving chase.

"The bag," shouted Noggin to Fitz pointing at the two pirates trying to keep their feet whilst hanging onto the bag with all their might. "It's full of Nightmare Pearls, be careful they mustn't break open."

Darting across the sky the dragons began to surround the ship. Filling their giant lungs, they rained blasts of fire at the masts and sails trying to bring the ship down.

Without warning, a blizzard of driving snow appeared as they passed the snow covered villages of the Frost Fairies, Ice Imps, and the Hail Hurlers. The flames on the burning masts and sails went out like a light leaving only trails of smoke and charred remains.

Chunks of ice pounded the ship and bounced off the dragon's scales as the Hail Hurlers joined the battle. With hail settling on the deck it became a skating rink as the Frost Fairies and Ice Imps turned it to sheets of ice. Slowly the sails began to stiffen making the ship slow down.

"Keep going they're beginning to freeze," shouted Bysidian as he and his men tried in vain to board the rocking ship.

With the pirates skidding all over and the captain busy trying to hold onto the wheel no one noticed the red and white dragons flying below the ship's bow.

"Steady Ember, steady," said Fitz as he climbed from his seat and stood on her back. The wind and snow were so powerful they almost blew him over as the cold ran down his neck numbing his face and ears. Reaching out he grabbed the carved figurehead and pulled himself up.

"Here give me your hand," he said to Nift as he pulled her from Moonstone to join him.

They flew out of the snowstorm away from the cold and gradually the helpers from the villages of snow and ice were gone.

"We have to find that bag and quickly," said Fitz as they climbed along the figurehead and dropped onto the ship's deck.

The ice had begun to melt, and the pirates were too busy trying to drop the burnt sails to notice a couple of extras onboard.

As they reached Dolomite Dell the ship crashed into the treetops, ripping branches off and raining down leaves on the tiny houses below. Cowering in their homes the Dream Drifters watched the shadow of the ship turn the streets black as it passed overhead.

"We're almost at Cloud Bay, they mustn't get there with the bag of pearls" called Bysidian to his men.

"How do we stop them the dragons can't get anywhere near the ship for us to land?" asked Templar Storm.

"All we need is to get that bag. You heard him if he escapes with those nightmares, he intends to use them for an army."

"Argent get as close as you can, I can jump to that mast. I may have a huge fight on my hands, but we have to stop those Nightmare Pearls leaving this island. Noggin hold on tightly to Argent she will keep you safe."

As Argent swooped above the fleeing ship it swayed left then right as Solomon Fear turned the wheel to stop Bysidian getting near.

"I SEE YOU" he bellowed using the tall, burnt, wooden masts as weapons to keep the silver dragon

189

away. "BIG BRAVE NIGHT WARRIOR. WELL, YOU ARE NOT BOARDING THIS SHIP EVER."

A loud *THUD* on the deck behind made the unsuspecting captain turn sharply. Standing with their swords drawn and cloaks flapping in the wind were Templar Storm and Fabian Feldspar.

"Maybe you should concentrate on more than one dragon next time" smiled Fabian.

Solomon Fear drew his sword. "So that's how it is hey? Sneaking up whilst I was distracted with my brother's stupid bravery. I can take two of you with my hands tied. I trained you remember?"

The pirate crew around them started to close in, swords and daggers glinting in their hands, ready to protect their precious captain.

"NO," said Solomon Fear "these two are mine, back away." With a clash of swords and cheers from his crew, Solomon Fear charged at the two Night Warriors. As their blades met every pirate on the ship turned to watch their brave captain defeat the Night Warriors.

"Oh, this could get nasty," said Three-Toes Magee straining his neck over the crowd. "I can't see a thing, can you?"

"Nope not a thing, hang on a moment," said Boz-Eyed Bert as with a *pop* he pulled out one of his wonky eyes and held it high. "Ah, there we go I can see nice and clear now."

"Ugh, that is soooo gross" wailed Three -Toes "I wish you wouldn't do that it freaks me out every time. Look I've goose bumps all over me."

"Well at least I can see what's happening, you're only jealous," replied Bert. "If you think that's gross you should see what I see when both eyes stop facing into my head."

The pirates in front of them stumbled backwards as the captain jumped to avoid a sword swipe.

"MY EYE," wailed Bert as it was knocked from his hand and sent flying across the deck. "Quick it's rolling away, watch your feet" he snapped to the pirates around him.

"That'll teach you for showing off" laughed Three-Toes as he went to help his friend.

"Hold on, it's coming your way," called Bert as they chased the eye back and forth across the deck and away from the pirate crowd. "There it is, grab it quick."

"I've got my hands full, hang on" replied Three-Toes as he put the bag of stolen pearls down and grabbed for the eye rolling towards him. He watched with horror as it rolled straight between his feet and bounced down the stairs behind him to the galley below.

"You knuckleheaded nincompoop" wailed Bert, "come on get after it" as they both charged down the stairs.

"Now's our chance come on" whispered Fitz as the abandoned bag slid side to side across the deck. They snuck across the ship keeping one eye on the bag and one on the pirates. From way above Noggin saw them "look Bysidian, look," she said pointing them out.

"HOORAY" came the cheer as Solomon Fear swiped the sword from Fabian's hand, but like lightning, he turned to catch it. With the sword returned to his hand, he saw Fitz and Nift reaching for the bag.

"Come on Solomon is that all you've got?" he laughed out loud keeping the pirate's attention firmly on him.

"Got it, come on" whispered Fitz as he grabbed the bag and ran, but voices started to get louder from the staircase to below deck and they stopped in their tracks.

193

"Well look at the state of it, did you have to kick it under that table. It's scratching like an itchy scratchy thing."

"Oh, that will be the rat hair, old toenails and bits of crusty bogies, I did try to rub them off before you put it back in" came the reply.

Three-Toes and Boz-Eye walked out onto the deck and stopped as they stood face to face with Fitz and Nift.

"Hey, what do think you're doing?" cried Three-Toes. "You little thieves, that's our bag, not yours give it back."

"We're only taking back what was ours to start with," said Fitz. "Do you know what's in here and what they can do?"

"Yeh shiny black pearls full of creepy things, real pretty they are, and the captain likes them so GIVE THEM BACK," said Bert.

"If you want them so bad then come and get them," said Nift with a grin as she and Fitz took off across the deck.

"Come here you little worms" cried Bert as he grabbed for Fitz.

"Over to you" called Fitz as he threw the bag to Nift. She ran on giggling as Three-Toes tripped over a rope and hit the deck.

"Oh, my nose, right you've had it" he snapped as he lunged for Nift. Like an acrobat, she dodged his hands and spun around tossing the bag to Fitz.

With no one at the wheel, the ship was rolling like a wild beast side to side as it arrived at Cloud Bay.

"Time to go," called Nift as they tried to stay steady on their feet, but as the ship clipped a chimney pot Fitz stumbled and the bag flew from his hands.

"NO," he cried scrambling to get to his feet, but he was not quick enough and as the two pirates and Nift all grabbed for the bag it became a tug of war.

"Let go it's ours" snapped Three-Toes pulling with all his strength.

"No, it's not, you stole it, let go yourself" replied Nift pulling back.

"Kick her in the shins Magee, we owe them a good shin kicking," said Bert as he tried to swing the bag around to make Nift let go.

"Don't you dare you stinking pirate" cried Fitz as he launched himself onto Bert's back and tried to pull him off. Push, pull, push, pull the bag began to tear as they struggled and moved towards the side of the ship.

"Pull Nift get it off him, hurry," said Fitz.

"I SAID LET GO" yelled Bert as he gave one final yank of the bag.

196

As the bag ripped in two it sent them all tumbling backwards. They watched in horror as the black Nightmare Pearls were flung into the air.

"NOOOOO" cried Fitz and Nift as they hung over the ship's side and watched the cluster of black swirling pearls plummet through the cloud sea below.

"WHAT HAVE YOU DONE YOU BLITHERING IDIOTS" screeched Solomon Fear as all the pirates turned towards the commotion, "DON'T JUST STAND THERE, GET THEM."

"Down here, hurry" yelled Noggin now aboard Ember. Without hesitation, Fitz and Nift jumped over the side of the ship and in a flash of red were gone.

Like a blur, Bysidian and the two Night Warriors watching from above shot past the ship and through the clouds chasing the falling pearls.

"Time to go" yelled Templar to Fabian as they rushed forward knocking Solomon Fear off his feet. Launching themselves over the side they landed in their dragon's saddles and joined the chase.

Scrambling back to his feet Solomon Fear grabbed the wheel and with a yell of anger, he turned the ship downwards towards the cloud sea and disappeared.

****

On the beach Ember, Moonstone and the Dream Drifters stood watching and waiting for what seemed like an eternity.

Eventually, with an explosion of white mist, the Night Warriors rose from the sea and without looking back flew to Dreamcast Mountain.

"Come on" yelled Fitz as they climbed aboard their dragons and followed. Bursting from the tunnel slides they ran down the passages where the monsters smell still lingered and giant spider's webs hung heading to the vaults.

Inside stood the High Minister and Bysidian Black, voices from the Nightmare Vault meant the other Night Warriors were close by.

"Did you get them?" asked Fitz as they burst into the vault "please tell me you found them?"

"We're not sure, we don't know how many he took, my men are looking now," said Bysidian. "We caught three, but they were scattered far and wide by the time we caught up to them."

"We had them, we had them in our hands. I'm so sorry," whispered Fitz hanging his head.

The High Minister walked over and placed a hand on his arm "Never be sorry, all of you were heroes. You protected everyone out there on the island and you never thought of your safety once.

We may not have the pearls but more importantly, neither does Solomon Fear."

From the shadows the Night Warriors walked towards them, Bysidian looked at them anxiously.

"Three gaps, not counting the one that burst open in the fight," said Quillion.

"Three," repeated Bysidian in a low voice looking at the High Minister. "We need to find them. You know he stole the strongest pearls, the ones with the worst nightmares imaginable inside, don't you?"

"Of course, he did" sighed the High Minister "I would expect nothing less."

"So, what are we waiting for?" asked Linc "if there are Nightmare Pearls out there, we need to find them."

"But how do we find them, they could be anywhere?" asked Snitch.

"We watch and we listen. Don't worry they'll appear and when they do, we will call," said the High Minister shuffling away.

****

As Ember dropped into Dolomite Dell, Fitz, Noggin, and Snitch were silent. Weary with disappointment, aching, cut and bruised from the battle they said their goodnights and headed home to bed.

Days and nights passed, and slowly the island returned to normal. More nightmares were caught and locked away, and more happy dreams were left under pillows.

Solomon Fear and his men had gone, searching for his stolen pearls no doubt and the fog down on

Earth, well it seemed to have a strange lavender scent.

No word came of the lost pearls.

As the moon rose and shone through his bedroom window Fitz clambered out of bed. Unable to sleep he opened his window wide and looked out across Dolomite Dell. The distant thuds of bouncing beetles and the plinking of glass frogs were the only sounds in the darkness as a rainbow coloured slug slipped across his windowsill.

"Where are you?" he whispered with a sigh before turning to climb back under the covers.

Without warning a blast of powerful wind blew through the open window almost blowing Fitz off his feet. Turning Fitz came face to face with Bysidian Black aboard Argent hovering outside his window.

"We found one"….

Watch out for these other titles …

If you have a moment to spare, please leave a review on
Amazon.
Your help with spreading the world of the Dream Drifters
would be greatly appreciated.

dianebanhamimagine@outlook.com
Facebook @DianeBanhamAuthor
Instagram @dianebanham

Printed in Poland
by Amazon Fulfillment
Poland Sp. z o.o., Wrocław